CHARLIE AND THE WHITE HOUSE

For my wife Yuan
and children Sylvia, Olivia

By Yaoxiang WANG

Some of the comments by friends and readers who have had a preview of the manuscript

- A long-awaited book that has finally been completed. Not only children but also adults who have read the other two books about Charlie will find it very interesting and entertaining.

- A well written novel with a lively imagination, an attractive plot and a keen sense of humour. I could hear myself laughing when I was reading some of the paragraphs.

- Will certainly be another classic for children's literature.

- Can't believe it was written by a non-native English speaker. Really amazed by the way the story was unfolded and his great sense of humour.

- One of the most attractive, funniest novels I have ever read in recent years. We should all put away our cell phones and take time to read it. Wish a movie could be made one day based on the novel.

- Can hardly imagine what Roald DAHL will say if he reads the novel. Can they work together to produce the fourth book in the series?

Table of Contents

1 A DULL Fan

2 The Original Manuscript Found

3 Special Fudgemallow Delights

4 Off to the White House

5 MBA

6 Fudgemallow Delights Took Effect

7 Shopping for Clothes

8 The Welcome Ceremony on the North Lawn

9 In the Guest Rooms

10 The Press Conference

11 The Welcome Banquet

12 Second day in the White House

13 The Underground Pentagon

14 Starting all over again

15 The Vulnerable Moment

16 Talk with the Real President

17 The **Grand** Decision

18 The Farewell Dinner

19 Contract for Fudgemallow Delights

20 Flying Back Home

References

About the author

Other books (Wong boks) by Yaoxiang WANG

1 A DULL Fan

When I was a little child, I just loved reading Roald DAHL's novels, "The Magic Finger", "Fantastic Mr Fox", "George's Marvellous Medicine", "Esio Trot", "James and the Giant Peach", "The BFG", "The Witches", not to mention the well-known "Charlie and the Chocolate Factory" and "Charlie and the Great Glass Elevator".

Throughout my childhood, I had a few different bookshelves in my compact but cosy bedroom, but his books were always placed at my eye level on the shelf so that I could always look at them whenever I walked past them. The mere glimpse of his books on the shelf brought me great joy and pleasure.

Every night, I would take one of his books from the bookshelf and place it under my pillow before I went to bed, hoping I would become one of the fascinating characters in his books and have some marvellous and memorable experience, like George in "George's Marvellous Medicine", or James in "James and the Giant Peach", or Sophie in "The BFG".

My bedroom was, and still is, decorated with his posters. By posters, I mean enlarged colour photocopies of his book covers as there were no posters available for his fans or readers at that time. If you have a chance to visit my bedroom, you will see that every inch of the walls and the ceiling is covered with the posters except the windows. Every time my mother showed my bedroom to her visitors who were interested to see the entire house, she would say, "What a waste of my hard-earned money spent on those expensive wallpapers!"

Tell me a DAHL's book that I don't know and I will pay you ten times as much as you earn every day. I can remember every detail of all his novels and even all those new and peculiar words that he coined for his novels such as *vermicious, jumpsquiffling, trogglehumper, gloriumptious,* etc.etc.

I was so indulged in his books that I even wanted to change my last name to DULL, so that it would sound like and rhyme with DAHL. But my father, who was, in actual fact, a very funny school teacher at that time, didn't approve the idea as he didn't want to be called Mr DULL by his students.

The last two DAHL's books I read when I was a little boy were "Charlie and the Chocolate Factory" and "Charlie and the Great Glass

Elevator". As soon as I finished reading them, I asked my father whether or not there existed a third book in the series about Charlie as the story didn't seem to be finished. He said there was indeed a third book which was called "Charlie and the White House", but he added that unfortunately DAHL, for one reason or another, was never able to finish the book. I thought he was not telling me the truth as he didn't want to give me more pocket money to buy the book, so before we could end our conversation, I dashed to the nearby bookshop to see if it was available. I was so disappointed and dismayed and *distravengated* when I was told by the bald and skinny yet polite and knowledgeable sales assistant that DAHL never wrote more than the first chapter of the book.

How could that be possible? I couldn't believe my ears. I couldn't buy his words. I couldn't trust him just as I couldn't trust the weather forecast or politicians. I still couldn't believe that was the truth even though everyone else told me the same story when I came back home. How can you easily believe what people say? As you can obviously see, even the word bel**ie**ve has got a **lie** in it.

It is my instinct and intuition that the manuscript must be somewhere in DAHL's brick writing hut on the edge of the orchard at Gipsy House at Great Missenden just outside London in the Buckinghamshire village. It is highly plausible that his family members or close relatives were not able to find it. Or it might have been misplaced somewhere in the hut, for example, in the wastepaper basket which has not been touched since then and it is still covered by other discarded waste. Or DAHL's lovely and helpful secretary, Wendy, has still got those piles and piles of his yellow scribbled paper to be sent to his publisher. Or DAHL must have hidden his manuscript somewhere in his hut either because he didn't wish to publish the third book in the series anymore for some reason or because he intended to completely rewrite the book or because he planned to give his readers and fans a huge surprise in thirty years' time.

As a little child, I knew by my aptitude that the manuscript was there, but I didn't have time and resources to search for it. Now that I have just become an adult and have a long holiday ahead of me and with patience and all the money that I have saved hard over the years, I am determined to find out the truth myself. I know I might not be as lucky as Charlie who received a full truck load of chocolate from Mr WONKA, but at least I might be as **rich** as the scrumptious chocolate that Charlie has in possession as people always say, men and chocolate, they both have to be **rich**.

2 The Original Manuscript Found

So, one day, a day that I have been waiting for so long, I joined a tourist group to visit Roald's brick writing hut on the edge of the orchard at Gipsy House at Great Missenden just outside London in the Buckinghamshire village. After a long flight followed by a long drive the next day, we finally arrived at the destination. The hut was painted white with a yellow front door. It was full of gadgets: a chair with a hole cut out on the back to prevent pressure on his damaged spine, a writing board of exactly the right thickness, tilted at exactly the right angle and an old suitcase filled with logs for a footrest, a green sleeping bag where he could tuck up his legs, a rickety old electric fire on two parallel wires on the ceiling he rigged up so he could pull it towards him if his fingers got cold. The hut still stood exactly as Roald left it, with everything set up ready for writing. His cigarettes ends were in the ashtray. It was as if he had just popped out for a bit.

The above description of his hut was taken from one of Roald's published books. I could not find or create a better or more precise description than that as the hut was in exactly the same condition and status as depicted when I saw it with my very own eyes.

Let's continue with my incredible experience. While I was looking around in the hut, I felt I had to make use of the restroom at the back of his hut as I ate too much fruit and drank too much herbal tea at the hotel which provided a scrumptious buffet breakfast in the morning. As I pushed the button twice to flush the toilet after use (By the way, two is my lucky number and I always do everything with two, e.g. when I knock on the door, when I beep the horn, when I stomp my foot, etc. and I would certainly call it a **royal flush** as my last name, WANG, means king), the decorative painting hung above the toilet slid to the left quietly and miraculously and a cavity the size of a bedside table appeared. This must be Roald's secret hoard! I was so flabbergasted by the scene and stood there speechless and motionless for a whole minute before I could take a deep breath, calm down, and decided to have a good look at what was inside.

In the dim torch light from my phone, I was able to see quite a few containers, which were made of different materials, in different shapes and colours scattered all over the hole. I could not wait to open the first one that I saw and grabbed in my hand. It was a wooden box of dark walnut colour and when I pulled out the yellow pile of paper, I could immediately tell with no doubt that it was the original manuscript of "Charlie and the Chocolate Factory". Next to the walnut wooden box stood a glass jar and I could already see clearly that it was the manuscript of "Charlie and the Great Glass Elevator" before I plucked it out. My heart was pounding fast and my adrenaline was pumping up as I opened the third white marble container with trembling hands. Eureka! The complete manuscript of the first chapter of "Charlie and the White House" and some scribbled notes for the rest of the book that perhaps no one would be able to read except Roald himself and his secretary Wendy.

There were a few more other containers at the back of the cavity but I didn't care or bother at all. That was the very one I had been searching for. That was exactly the very one I had been craving. I browsed through the first chapter of the book in a blink and found out that it was entirely different to the chapter that is being displayed at Roald Dahl Museum and Story Centre. "Oh my goodness! Good gracious me!" I kept on saying those as I thumbed through the pages of the manuscript. I immediately realised that the first chapter known to the public might have been written by a professional writer who imitated DAHL's writing style to fool the readers and the fans.

I almost gave out a scream and tended to rush out with the manuscript to show my exciting discovery to the people still looking around in the hut or waiting outside the hut to travel to the next scenic spot. Then, I froze and thought, what if DAHL's posterity didn't wish to publish the third book in the series anymore? What if they intended to keep everything as it is? What would they do to me if they knew I had discovered the secret?

I could hear the tourist guide shouting right outside the hut in her usual dull voice, "We are leaving the premises in five minutes. We are leaving the premises in five minutes. Please wait right outside the hut when you are ready. Thank you!"

I knew I would not be able to take anything out of the hut as everyone went past a scanner which took a record of all our personal belongings before we entered this well preserved and protected private property. What could I do? What should I do? My mind raced quickly. When I saw my phone in my hand used as a torch, I suddenly had an idea. Yes, I could take photographs of the manuscript and the notes. I quickly placed the manuscript and the notes on the floor and took photographs of every page of the manuscript and the notes with the assistance of the flashlight. Some of the paragraphs and pages were blurred and damaged due to moisture and condensation as the pile of the yellow scribbled paper had been sitting in the container for almost fifty years, but that didn't matter. The remaining battery percentage of my phone was 1% when I had completed the task. I put the manuscript back to its white marble container swiftly and pressed the flush button twice to conceal the hole with the painting and joined the rest of the tourist group waiting anxiously for me outside the hut.

As soon as I caught sight of the guide in the crowd, I went up to her and told her that I would like go back to the hotel by myself immediately and therefore would not be able to see the rest of the scenic attractions and go shopping with them in the afternoon as previously arranged in the itinerary. However, I would have dinner with the rest of the tourist group when they came back in the evening. The guide did not seem to be supportive of my idea but finally gave her consent when she sensed that I was adamant about my decision.

Without any further delay, I contacted a book publishing company to find out whether or not they would publish the book if and when I completed it based on the original notes that I discovered and of which I took photographs. They were so thrilled to hear the news. When the publishers received the completed book in about three months' time, they said they could hardly **put it down** (in fact they told me they thought at the very first beginning they would have to **put up with it**) and assured me that it would be one of the best sellers of the year.

So here is the third book in the series, "Charlie and the White House" with notes and ideas taken from DAHL's original manuscript.

3 Special Fudgemallow Delights

The pilot who had been assigned to come and pick up the eight astronauts did not bother to switch off the engine after he landed successfully adjacent to the factory gate. People gathering around the gate virtually had to shout and scream if they wanted to talk to one another. When he caught sight of Mr WONKA, Charlie, his parents and his four grandparents dancing out of the factory with their arms linked together, he shouted at the top of his lungs, "Hello! Our most lespectable heloes and heloines!" The pilot, who was not a native speaker of English, tended to replace the "r" sound with the "l" sound when he spoke. "I am gleatly honoured to have been assigned by Mr Plesident to take you to the White House. Are we all leady to go?"

Mr WONKA shouted back with a smile as well as an apologetic look on his face, "Oh, sorry! Just a minute, please. I am terribly sorry that I forgot to bring the WONKA fudgemallow delights with me for Mr President."

He then shrieked to Charlie who was standing right beside him, "Hey, Charlie, can you go back to the factory with me to help fetch the fudgemallow delights?" Without waiting for an answer from Charlie, he turned quickly to the others and cried out, "While we go back to get the fudgemallow delights, the rest of you may start boarding the helicopter."

He dragged Charlie back to where they were and as soon as both of them were inside the factory, Mr WONKA said, "Charlie, I am really excited! This is a once in a lifetime opportunity. Not many people have the chance and pleasure to meet the President. Imagine a photograph with him with his autograph! He is really grateful to us for saving the capsule and may even grant us three wishes. What will you wish for, Charlie?"

"My three wishes have already come true," Charlie replied. "I have bought the chocolate bar with the gold ticket. I have been invited to visit your chocolate factory and as a result, I have seen and known all the secrets and magic of the factory. I have been given enough chocolate and sweets which will last for the rest of my life. What else should I wish for?"

"Are you sure you don't have any more wishes?"

"Well, if you really want me to have three more wishes, I …… I just wish that I could share and enjoy happily and *burrily* all the chocolate and sweets with my family and friends who would never be sick or die. That we could have peace forever and ever. And that we could all love one another." Charlie answered after he thought for a little while.

"Well, if you cannot love **one another**, just interchange the last two words", said Mr WONKA with a grin. "But seriously, it's pretty tough, Charlie. Think of that. The US President is in control of thousands and thousands of missiles and numerous nuclear and chemical weapons. With the secret code that he, or to be exact, one of his assistants, carries all the time wherever they go and the pressing of a few buttons, he can effortlessly have the earth totally destroyed a dozen times."

Charlie was obviously a bit frightened upon hearing that. He was hesitant to ask Mr WONKA, "Then would I be able to make a request to the President to destroy all the life threatening missiles and nuclear and chemical weapons when we meet him?"

"I am afraid not", Mr WONKA sighed helplessly. "Even if he agrees to do so, the presidents of the other countries the possess nuclear and chemical weapons will not follow suit. And if they won't, the President will have no desire or intention to do so. We are in a vicious and *vermiotrocious* cycle as you can see."

"Then I really wish all the detestable missiles and weapons could be destroyed. I wish we could all enjoy love and peace on earth. Do you have any magic formula for that?" Charlie asked anxiously, looking pleadingly and anxiously into Mr WONKA's eyes.

"I don't know. I know time is pressing, but I think we could make some 'special' WONKA fudgemallow delights for Mr President. This is the only chance that we can do something to change the world and I need your ideas and help."

"But how can fudgemallow delights destroy the missiles and weapons just like how can I, Charlie, a little boy, destroy a mountain?"

Mr WONKA gave out a chuckle, "Of course you can't. But you can if you've got magic power. We don't have time to talk about the details now. We have to act quickly. The pilot and your parents and your grandparents are waiting for us anxiously outside and they don't want to wait too long. Now listen! In one of my cupboards down in my hexagon office at the other end of the factory, I have some very special ingredients which I have never used for my chocolate before. I will make use of them now to make some special fudgemallow delights for Mr President. While I go quickly to fetch them, can you scoop some chocolate from the flowing and bubbling waterfall and get them ready for making the fudgemallow delights? I'll be back in a jiffy."

"Sure thing." Charlie replied with a smile and started walking towards the waterfall without delay. He could hear the Oompa Loompas who had already arrived to help him make the fudgemallow delight singing joyfully.

Our dear Mr WONKA and Charlie Bucket and his family
Have been invited by the American President Lancelot R. Gilligrass
Not because of the scrumptious chocolate bars or brownie
But because they saved the transport capsule in an elevator made of glass

But before they go to meet the President in the White House
They will fabricate some special fudgemallow delights in the factory
From ingredients stored in Mr WONKA's office infested with a mouse
To serve as desserts and celebrate the unrivalled victory

So now let's have a look at the mysterious ingredients
That are to be used for making the fudgemallow delights
They have been handed down to Mr WONKA from his great great grandparents
And have been boiled and cooked in the cauldron for a hundred days and nights

Hind legs of a gerenuk and spots of a wunderpus photogenicus
Leaves from linaria vulgaris and flowers from sempervivum tectorum
Paws of a pink fairy armadillo and barks from anigozanthos flavidus
Ears of a gobi jerboa and seeds from chenopodium album

Pollens from dicentra eximia and tassels of a wobbegong
Feet of a patagonian mara and pelvic fins of a lumpsucker
Veins of a sunda colugo and ligaments of a dugong
Stems from aralia spinosa and tails of a hellbender

*What magic can these wonderful fudgemallow delights exactly do
We haven't got the foggiest idea and cannot give you any tips
You will find out when they are served to Mr President and his crew
As well as to the others including the Vice President Miss Elvira Tibbs*

Mr WONKA dashed to his hexagon office like an athlete, flung open the door and then his cupboard, quickly lifted the lid off a metal box, snatched a sachet and hurried his way back to Charlie.

With the help of the Oompa Loompas, the fudgemallow delights had already taken shape in the moulds when Mr WONKA returned.

"Well done, Charlie!" exclaimed Mr WONKA as he tore open one of the sachets and sprinkled the contents evenly onto the surface of the freshly made fudgemallow delights. The magic powder melted with the warm and *keleany* chocolate and sank deep into the fudgemallow delights which were soon ready to be packed up. Again, with the help of the Oompa Loompas as well as Mr WONKA, Charlie quickly wrapped them up and arrayed them beautifully in two large containers.

"Yippee! Let's go", Mr WONKA dragged Charlie by his left arm and they dashed towards the helicopter waiting outside the gate of the factory.

4 Off to the White House

By the time Mr WONKA and Charlie came out of the factory with two large parcels of fudgemallow delights enough to feed all the people in the White House, the rest of the heroes had already taken their spots in the helicopter. The pilot looked a bit impatient now although he still tried to sound politely, "Are we all leady to take off?" He had to yell at everybody as it was very hard to hear anything else except the propellers of the helicopter which were still spinning madly like an enormous fan.

"Yes, we are. Sorry to have kept you waiting." Both Mr WONKA and Charlie yelled back simultaneously as they boarded the helicopter which closed its door smoothly and rose into the blue sky slowly. Very soon it became a giant dragonfly heading towards the White House *spraurastically*.

"Mr Plesident. We are on our way now. Should be there in about thlee hours." The pilot spoke into the microphone protruding from one side of the helicopter.

Upon hearing that, Grandpa Joe, who was sitting two rows behind the pilot, quickly said to Charlie, "Charlie, can you tell the pilot to land on the roof of a big shopping mall on our way for us to do some shopping?"

Charlie nodded and went up to the pilot asking him if they could land on the roof of a big shopping centre on their way so that they could all pop downstairs to buy exactly what they wanted for the occasion, but the pilot replied adamantly, "Solly, no time for shopping. Mr Plesident and his men will be welcoming you light outside the White House in exactly thlee hours." He took a quick glance at the time displayed in the instrument panel, "In fact, in exactly two hours and fifty-four minutes."

"Charlie," Grandma Josephine wailed. "We cannot go to see Mr President like this. I want to get off!"

"No, we can't." Grandma Georgina agreed. "You all go and I will stay in the helicopter until someone brings me a decent outfit."

Charlie moved closer to Mr WONKA and said, "Mr WONKA. Can you please ask the pilot to stop over on the way, please? I totally agree with them. They cannot go to see Mr President like this. It is so embarrassing and *imunating*."

"And not respectful," Grandma Josephine and Grandma Georgia shouted at the same time.

Mr WONKA said, "No, he won't listen to anyone. He is just a pilot, an Air Force officer. He only does what he is told to do. He will be in big trouble if he disobeys the order."

"Mr WONKA. What about your magic fudgemallow delights?" Charlie's mind was racing quickly and he immediately thought of the magic power of the fudgemallow delights.

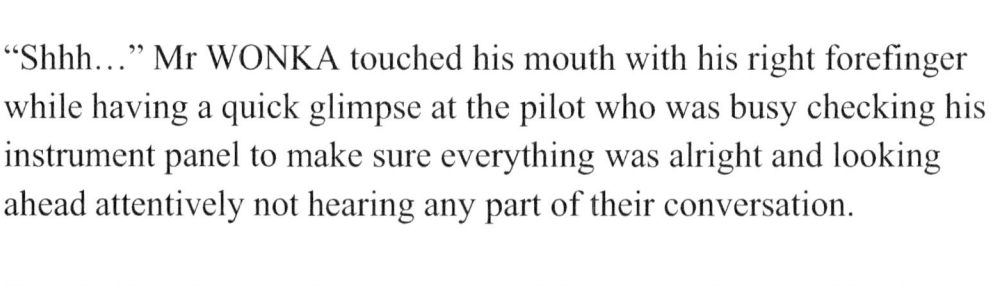

"Shhh…" Mr WONKA touched his mouth with his right forefinger while having a quick glimpse at the pilot who was busy checking his instrument panel to make sure everything was alright and looking ahead attentively not hearing any part of their conversation.

Slowly Charlie moved even closer to Mr WONKA and said to him in a whisper only loud enough for Mr WONKA to hear, "What can the fudgemallow delights do? Can you do something about it with them?"

5 MBA

"Well", replied Mr WONKA in a low voice that could only be heard by Charlie. "These special magic fudgemallow delights are called **MBA**, Middle Brain *Alterator*. They can alter or change or control your middle brain and in turn your entire brain."

"But we don't have middle brains." Charlie said, looking very perplexed. "I have never heard of middle brains. My dad said we only had left and right brain."

Mr WONKA looked and sounded like a scientist, a brain surgeon or a walking Wikipedia, "Yes. Of course we do, Charlie. The formal scientific name for middle brain is midbrain. The midbrain or mesencephalon (from the Greek mesos, middle, and enkephalos, brain) is a portion of the central nervous system associated with vision, hearing, motor control, sleep/wake, arousal (alertness), thoughts, actions and temperature regulation. The midbrain comprises the tectum (or corpora quadrigemina), tegmentum, the cerebral aqueduct (or ventricular mesocoelia or "iter"), and the cerebral peduncles, as well as several nuclei and fasciculi. Caudally the midbrain adjoins the metencephalon (afterbrain, pons and cerebellum); while rostrally it adjoins the diencephalon (thalamus, hypothalamus, etc.). The midbrain is located below the cerebral cortex, and above the hindbrain, placing it near the centre of the brain."

This was obviously too much for Charlie to understand and digest at his age. Mr WONKA was fully aware of that and he continued, "When I was a child, my grandfather asked my great great grandfather, who was 150 years old then, to create this special powder for me and named it MBA."

"What can it do?" Charlie became even more curious, interested and excited although still not being able to fully comprehend the concept of midbrain. "Well, as I said, it can alter or change or control your middle brain which in turn will control your entire brain." Mr WONKA tried to explain the concept again. This time, in a more simple and plain language that Charlie could understand. "The moment you chew and swallow the fudgemallow delights, the magic powder will quickly dissolve and be absorbed by your body, travelling into your blood vessels just like the extra sugar that will go into your blood vessels if you cannot produce sufficient insulin to absorb it. Then the powder will find its way to your middle brain via the blood vessels that are connected to the brain. Once the powder reaches your middle brain, it will start to affect the central nervous system, and thus control the entire brain.

Charlie, totally new to that concept, was now bombarding Mr Wonda with one question after another just like a child who would keep on asking what would happen next when listening to an exciting and fascinating story full of suspenses. "How do you know that the magic powder is taking effect and working properly for the person who takes it?"

Mr WONKA didn't lose any of his patience at all. "Usually it takes about four hours for the powder to have the full effect although it varies from person to person." He went on to say, "One mnemonic for remembering the structures of the midbrain for medical students involves visualizing the mesencephalic cross-section as an upside down bear face. The two red nuclei are the eyes of the bear and the cerebral crura are the ears. The tectum is the chin and the cerebral peduncles are the face and ears. The funny and interesting thing is, the face of the person who takes the special fudgemallow delights will start to resemble a bear face as well although in a very subtle way.

There will be light green marks on both cheeks, the eyes will become red and round, the mouth will be round as if the person is constantly singing a muted coloratura soprano, the chin will be W shaped as if there were two chins side by side."

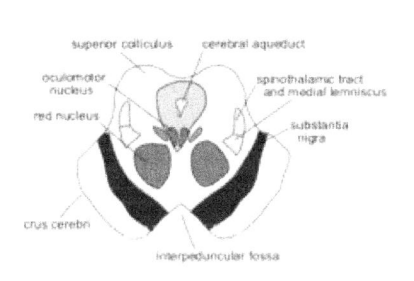

"The most important thing is," added Mr WONKA, "The first person who takes the powder will have the power to control the next person who takes it. The second person who takes it will have the power to control the person who takes it after him, and so on and so forth. If two or more people take it at the same time, they will have no power to control one another but will be controlled by the person who takes it before him."

Charlie, who now had a better grasp of the magic powder, was interested to find out more details about how the magic powder worked, "Can the top person control the people three or four levels down the line?

"Yes, absolutely. The top person is able to control any people at any levels. And what's more, as long as the interval between the two people who take them is less than 5 minutes, they will be at the same level."

"So, Mr WONKA, why don't you take it first to be at the top level before anyone else takes it by accident?" Charlie thought quickly and anxiously.

"Brilliant idea." Before Mr WONKA could finish his sentence, Charlie had already opened one of the containers and took a fudgemallow delight out of it.

Charlie gave it to Mr Wonda but he handed it back to Charlie and said, "No, you have it."

"But you need to have it first to be at the top level!" Charlie cried out loudly, totally forgetting that this should be a private and *resternable* conversation.

"Shhh…" Mr WONKA put his index finger on his mouth again, signalling to Charlie to lower his volume. "I took one ages ago but have never tried it out on someone. I want you to take this one so that you will be the next person to take it. So when I get old and pass beyond the veil of this world, you will be the top person in the pyramid."

"I see and thank you Mr WONKA." Charlie had no doubt in believing Mr WONKA now as he could see the subtle similarity of Mr WONKA's face to that of a bear, with light green cheeks, red and round eyes, a round mouth and a "W" shaped chin. He held the fudgemallow delight in front of him carefully and gratefully, looked at it for almost half a minute, and then put it into his mouth slowly with a strong determination.

Once the fudgemallow delight went down from his throat to his stomach through the esophagus, Charlie asked Mr WONKA, "What if we give one to the pilot? He will then be taking our order in his mind without even knowing it and will be too happy to land on the top of a shopping mall for us to do some shopping. We should test it out!"

"No, Charlie. They are meant to be gifts for Mr President and his men, special and extraordinary gifts especially prepared for them." Mr WONKA raised his voice a little bit. "Didn't you wish for peace and love? This might be the only opportunity we can seize to make sure that Mr President and his men take them."

Charlie was sad to hear that remark and he went back to his seat slowly and quietly. Grandpa Josephine and Georgina were still whinging and complaining and *trepolenting* near the pilot who was looking ahead with a serious facial expression.

The flight to the White House, like any other journeys, was so tedious and boring with the nonstop roaring of the engine blended with the loud noise of the spinning propellers that Grandpa Joe and Grandpa George started to doze off and so did Mr WONKA. Charlie had no time to worry about the gifts for Mr President and his men. All he was thinking was that he must get the helicopter to land on a shopping mall soon. Curiously and more importantly he wanted to find out if the magic fudgemallow delights would work as Mr WONKA said. So when he noticed that Mr WONKA was enjoying his nap, he took the chance to open one of the containers quickly and quietly. He then took out a fudgemallow delight with his fingers silently and went to the pilot who was flying the helicopter conscientiously in the front.

"Hi! How are you today? Would you like to try the new fudgemallow delight from Mr WONKA's chocolate factory?" Charlie said to the pilot casually and naturally, handing out the fudgemallow delight to him.

"Yes, I would love to." The pilot replied back, still looking a ahead with a stern look. He held out his hand and Charlie put the fudgemallow delight in his palm. Without even taking a look at it, the pilot tried to insert it all into his mouth. The size was a bit too big to push it all into his mouth so one third of it could still be seen between his lips. "Thanks. Tastes gleat." he said with a smile. Charlie took a photo of the pilot as he thought he really looked funny with the half protruding fudgemallow in his mouth.

There was a mild jerk due to a strong current and all those who were dozing off suddenly woke up. The pilot was still chewing the fudgemallow delight in his mouth and Mr WONKA could clearly see his chewing action from behind. Mr WONKA immediately realized what had happened. He opened the container swiftly and the missing fudgemallow delight confirmed his guess. He signalled Charlie to come over immediately.

"Charlie, my dear Charlie," Mr WONKA said worriedly in a low voice that could only be heard between the two of them. "You have messed up everything. First of all, now that the pilot has taken the fudgemallow delight first, he will be able to control Mr President and in turn all his men. Second, I told you it takes about 4 hours for the fudgemallow delight to take effect. The powder is like traditional Chinese medicine. It works, but slowly and surely. I reiterate. Charlie, you have messed up everything. You have messed up our plan. The whole plan. The entire plan. And I don't have Plan **Bee** or Plan **Sea**."

"Mr WONKA," Charlie said calmly. "With your second point, if it takes 4 hours for the fudgemallow delight to take effect, can't we prescribe triple dose by giving him two more so it will only take about one hour and twenty minutes for them to take effect? I am sure he wouldn't mind having two extra ones. With your first point, I think Plan A will still work. But let's worry about your second point first."

"Charlie", Mr WONKA exclaimed, "What would we do without you? You are brilliant. You are superb. But what about Plan A?"

"Trust me, Mr WONKA. We don't need Plan **Bee** or Plan **Sea**. I will brief you later. Let's continue with our plan A anyway."

In a flash, Charlie took out two more fudgemallow delights and offered them to the pilot, "Would you like some more? You like them, don't you? There will be plenty fudgemallow delights left for Mr President and his men."

"Sure. I was actually tlying to ask if I could have some more. It was so delicious and *plenautry*." The pilot glanced at Charlie with a smile, took the two fudgemallow delights and devoured them ravenously in no time.

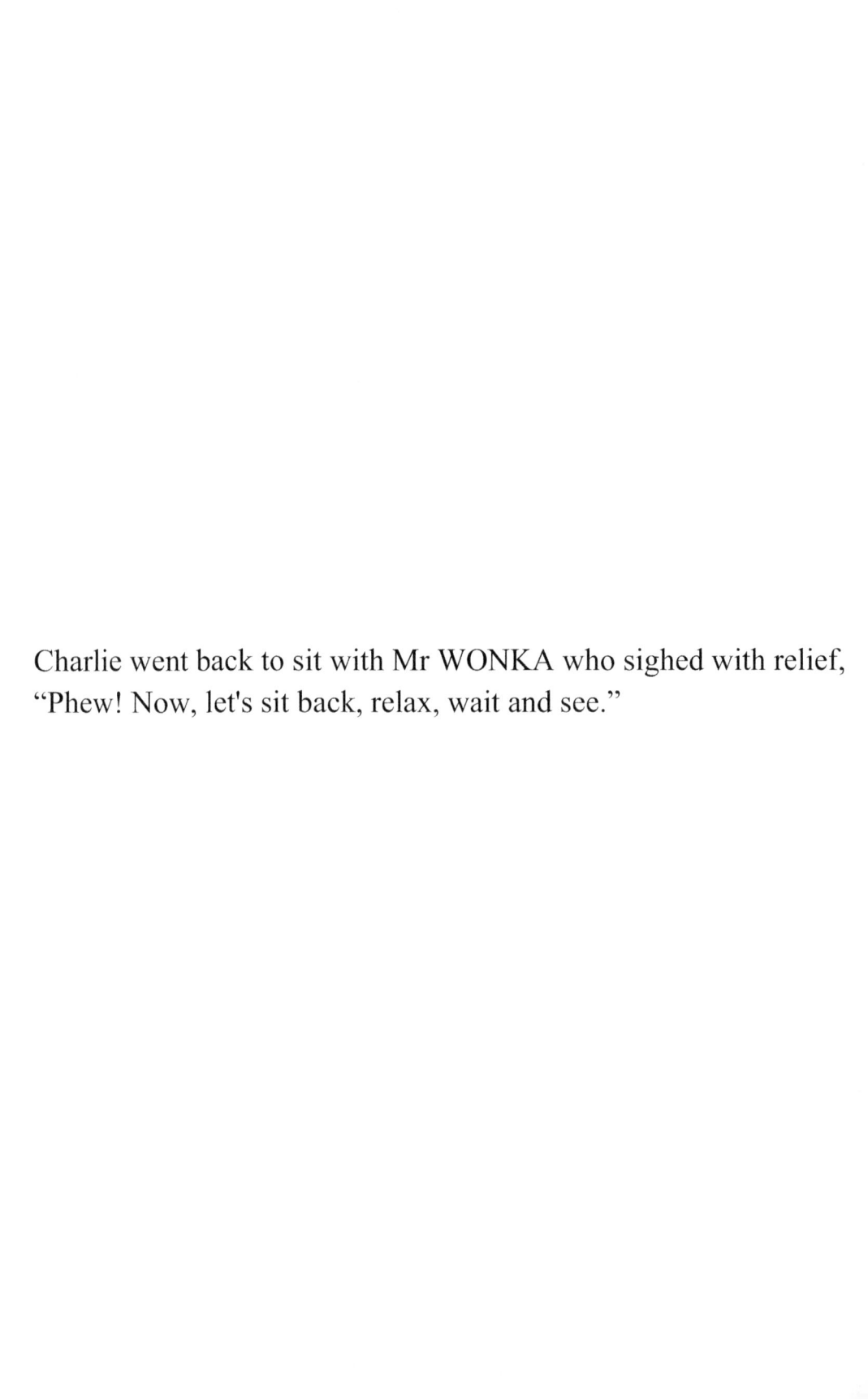

Charlie went back to sit with Mr WONKA who sighed with relief, "Phew! Now, let's sit back, relax, wait and see."

6 Fudgemallow Delights Took Effect

Time goes fast when you are having fun and always goes slowly when you are expecting something to happen. This one hour and twenty minutes were like **twenty-five hours and sixty-one minutes** to Charlie and Mr WONKA.

While waiting anxiously for the fudgemallow delights to take effect, Charlie asked Mr WONKA how the brain and the middle brain developed, obviously showing more interest in the human brain now.

Mr WONKA sounded once again like a medical expert, "The brain develops from neurons moving outward from early precursor cells. After the neurons move, they grow extensive dendrites (the input part of a neuron) and axons (the neuron's outputs). These early stages are driven by genetic instruction."

He paused for a while, took a glimpse at the pilot and continued, "Cells in the brain -- called gray matter -- develop throughout childhood and adolescence and then decrease in number. The axonal connections -- called white matter -- develop into adulthood."

He paused again, taking another quick look at the pilot and went on, "During embryonic development, the midbrain arises from the second vesicle, also known as the mesencephalon, of the neural tube. Unlike the other two vesicles, the forebrain and hindbrain, the midbrain remains undivided for the remainder of neural development. It does not split into other brain areas, while the forebrain, for example, divides into the telencephalon and thediencephalon."

Charlie found it hard to fully understand all those medical jargons and terminology, but Mr WONKA, who was in the mood, continued with his profound medical lecture that perhaps only medical students or professionals could comprehend, "Throughout embryonic development, the cells within the midbrain continually multiply and compress the still-forming cerebral aqueduct. Partial or total obstruction of the cerebral aqueduct during development can lead to congenital hydrocephalus."

"How did you know all this?" Charlie could not help asking.

"I used to be a doctor." Mr WONKA said. "A long time ago." He then told Charlie his story of studying in a medical school, how he became a doctor and how he stopped to run the chocolate factory later.

They kept on talking and did not even notice the passage of the time. By the time Charlie looked at his watch, more than one hour had passed.

"Charlie," Mr WONKA said, "Go and take a photograph of the pilot!"

"What for?" Charlie did not know why Mr WONKA wanted him to take a photo of the pilot.

"Just go and take one and I will tell you later."

Charlie went to the front of the helicopter, aimed at the pilot, zoomed in and took a clear picture of him. The pilot looked a bit different now. Charlie thought he must be tired after flying the helicopter for almost ninety minutes.

He went back to Mr WONKA who said, "Now show me the two photos you took of the pilot."

"I only took one." Charlie replied.

"You have two. The one you just took and the one you took when the pilot had the fudgemallow delight in his mouth."

Charlie began to understand why Mr WONKA wanted to look at the two photos now. He was so excited and found the other photo without delay. His hands were a bit trembling and *shikling* when he looked at the photos and then handed the camera to Mr WONKA.

"Mr WONKA," Charlie had to keep his voice down to suppress his excitement, "It has worked! Look at his face. It has changed. He now has red and round eyes and a round mouth and looks like a bear now."

"I cannot **bear** his face." Mr WONKA said with a chuckle. "In about another 10 minutes, Charlie, I want you to order him in your mind to land on the first shopping mall that he sees. Now we just sit down, wait and see."

Charlie was so excited that he took off his watch and held it in his hand. He did not want to do anything else except watching the time go by. He was counting down in his mind and when it finally reached three, two, one, zero, he said in his mind like a secret prayer, "Dear pilot. I command you to land on the roof of the first shopping mall you come across so that we can do some shopping." He then waited to see what would happen next.

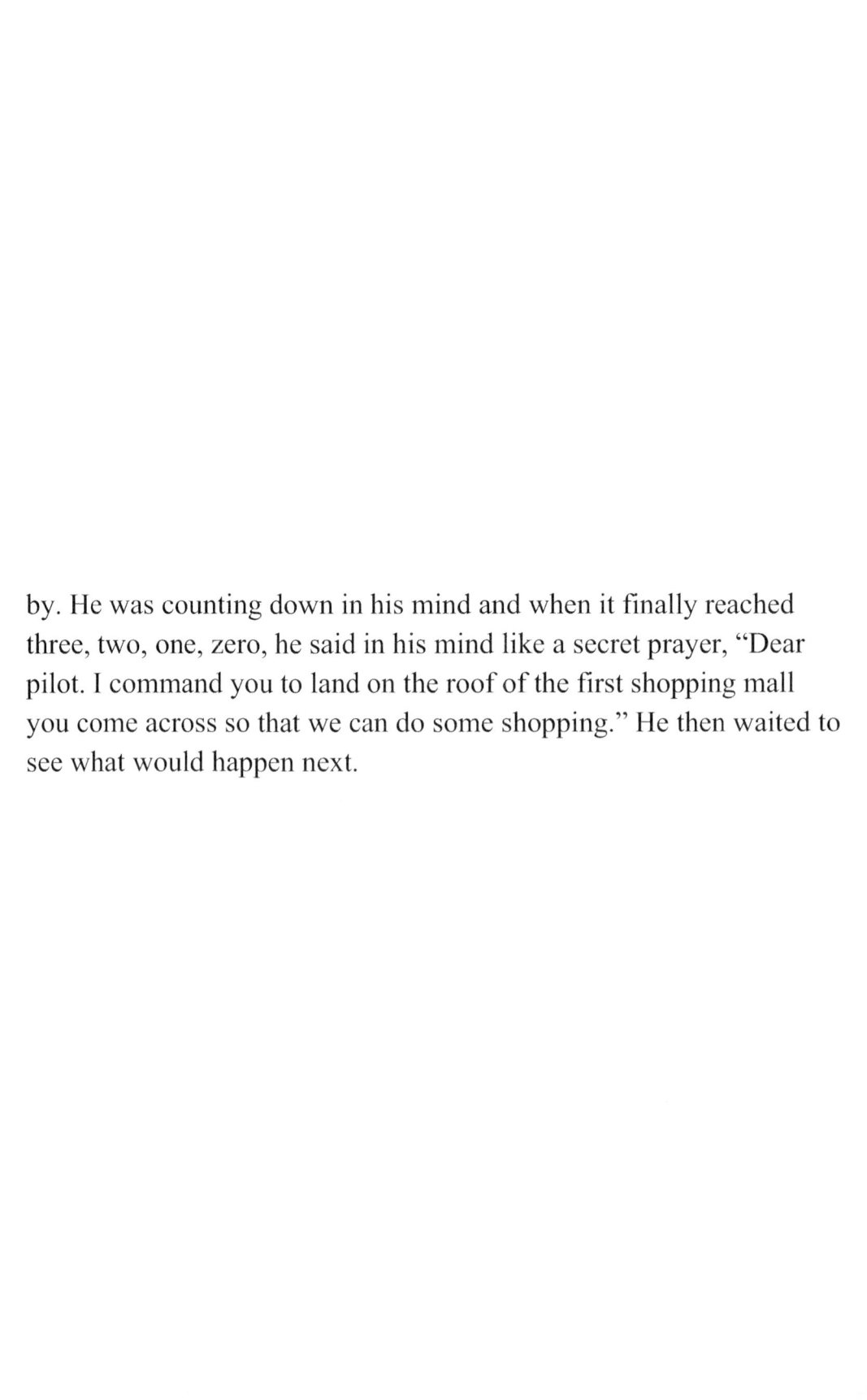

7 Shopping for Clothes

Just a few seconds after Charlie had said the command in his mind, a large shopping mall came into sight. One of the biggest that everyone on board had ever seen. Miraculously, the pilot turned around quickly and asked, "There is a big shopping mall ahead of us. Are you all happy if we just land on that one?"

Charlie could not believe what he heard. He looked at Mr WONKA who looked back at him with a chuckle and a thumb up.

Grandpa Joe and Grandpa George looked at their wives who were still sound asleep and shouted, "Hey ladies! Wake up! Did you hear what the pilot said? Do you want him to land on that shopping mall ahead of us?" Grandpa George tried to point at the shopping mall to show them but there was nothing ahead. "Where is it?"

"Behind us now", the pilot said with a grin.

Grandma Josephine and Grandma Georgina looked at the shopping mall behind them and shouted simultaneously, "Yes, of course. Yes, please. Thank you so much."

The helicopter came back in a circle and after a minute, it slowly descended and landed on the roof of the shopping mall. Mr WONKA, Charlie, Mr and Mrs Bucket, Grandpa Joe and Grandpa George got off the helicopter one after another.

"Come on, Grandma Josephine and Grandma Georgina." Charlie shouted at them.

"Sorry, we cannot leave the helicopter without being properly dressed. Can we get some decent clothes so that we can come out?" Grandma Georgina insisted.

"This is exactly what we are doing -- getting clothes for you ladies. You don't need to wear proper dresses to go and buy proper dresses. You are not seeing the President yet. Just the shop assistants."

"OK, OK. We are coming with you." The two Grandmas finally got off the helicopter still wrapped in towels and sheets.

It was indeed one of the biggest shopping malls in the world. It cut into the clear blue sky like a huge magnificent holy temple, casting a long and *dranadiac* shadow onto the earth around.

As they entered the mall, they came across a moving platform that ran along all the walkways in both directions just like the ones you see in the airports. There was a shuttle service from the far ends of the car parks to the entrance and food outlets were scattered throughout instead of being on one courtyard. There were professional shopping guides smiling at the customers at every entrance, always ready for more business.

It was the same temperature inside no matter what the season was. The light was the same, and so was the scent, the polished floor, the tense faces of the shoppers. Only the piped music and the fashions changed. People weren't people in there, they were consumers. They saw one another as obstacles -- both to walk around and wait behind for a turn to reach the tills. The only smiling faces were the ones who were selling. It was a friendly enough place if you had digits on your card, if you could line the pockets on the purveyors.

The clothing department was on the ground floor so they had to take an elevator to go downstairs. There were eight elevators and four escalators operating at the same time. Although Grandma Georgina and Josephine had travelled in the great glass elevator with the rest of the family before, they were still totally bewildered by the elevators in the mall. They saw old ladies their age go into the elevators and in a few seconds, out came some young and beautiful girls. They wanted to go into the very elevator that turned old ladies into young girls.

Charlie and Mr WONKA had to spend another 10 minutes explaining to them what an elevator in the shopping mall was like before they could head down to the clothing department.

"Look! There is a Walmart just over there. Let's just go there." Grandma Josephine shouted with excitement. All the shoppers around her turned their heads and looked at her.

"No," Mr WONKA said to Grandma Josephine, "They don't sell clothes to people who are going to meet the President. We need to find a decent shop for your clothes and I would pay for them."

So the group linked their arms again and marched along the shopping mall talking loudly and chanting joyfully. The other shoppers were all staring at them, wondering what was happening to this group of weird looking people and having no idea that this group of national heroes would meet the President very soon.

Just before they tried to turn around the corner in the mall, Mr WONKA saw a newly opened clothing shop. It was elegantly decorated and looked extremely extravagant. Mr WONKA went in and the rest of the group followed him.

"Welcome!" one of the shop assistants greeted them with her usual professional sweet smile. "How can I help you?"

"We want something to clothe ourselves." Grandma Georgina.

The shop assistant looked at the grandmas and tried very hard not to burst out laughing, "What sort of clothes are you exactly after?"

"I like eating leatherjacket fish so can I have a **leather jacket**, please?" Grandma Georgina said with a cheeky smile.

"And for me, a **coat of arms**, please." Grandma Josephine also joked, noticing Grandma Georgina was trying to be funny.

"Hahahaha." The shop assistant couldn't help laughing upon hearing their requests. "What about the pants to match them?"

"**Smarty pants**!" Both grandmas shouted concurrently and burst out laughing aloud.

"Come on, ladies, we have to be quick. No time for jokes" Mr WONKA had to interrupt them. He then turned to the shop assistant, "Please choose something suitable for these two ladies. Good enough for them to see some **VIPs**."

"You mean **Very Important Potatoes**?" Georgina was obviously still in the mood of joking.

The shop assistant took a few steps back, looked at the figures of the two grandmas and then went to the end of the shop where the beautiful and elegant dresses were stored. In a few seconds, she came back with two dresses hanging on both of her arms. "I hope these two will fit you and will be appropriate for the occasion." She said confidently with another smile.

The two grandmas went to the changing rooms and when they came out in a few minutes, they looked stunningly impressive and *gemanetic*. The two grandpas were looking at them with their mouths open as if they were looking at two brides. The two dresses were identical in colour and style and you could see that their gorgeous, fitted structure would cling to them hardly concealing anything. The sheer fabric glistened in the light, the flecks of gold in the luxurious champagne colour made them look a million dollar. The satin dresses glistened under the dimmed lights almost making it sparkle like the stars in the sky.

"Now we need matching shoes, matching handbags and matching jewelleries." The two grandmas shouted again simultaneously.

"Were your homes like **workshops** where the husbands **work** and the wives **shop**?" Mr WONKA asked the two grandpas. The humour from the two grandmas was contagious.

Mr WONKA ended up spending much more money on the accessories than on the dresses but he was delighted to see that the two ladies look so different and ecstatic in their glamorous new dresses.

"What about our beds?" Grandma Josephine put forward the same old question again.

"No, Grandma. Don't mention beds again." Charlie said. "There will be a lot of beds in the White House, much more than we need, and I am sure they will find a suitable one for you. Plus, there is no room in the helicopter to take your beds."

"Alright, alright. That will do. Let's go." The two grandmas replied back together again. They were so happy and excited and even Charlie, not good at singing at all, started to sing.

Today is the day for Grandma Georgina and Grandma Josephine
Who did their shopping in the world's biggest shopping mall
They asked for a coat of arms and smarty pants you must have seen
And they requested shoes and other accessories to match them all

Of course you all know they were merely kidding and joking
Because they were too thrilled and elated to conceal their excitement
They bought the fanciful dresses that the models were wearing
And shoes and accessories that matched so well to meet the President

The dresses were so beautiful and elegant and cost so much money
They looked as if they had been meticulously tailored to their need
The grandmas looked like two beautiful brides at a wedding ceremony
Although there was no accompanying best men or bridesmaids indeed

Imagine what the First Lady would think of the elegant dress
Visualize the reaction that the newspaper reporters would get
Envisage that the President might change his welcome address
Picture the surprise that the TV audience would never forget

Are they really Buckets' parents and Charlie's grandmas
Or are they supermodels that people see walking on the T stage
Are they shepherds and angels in the account of Christmas
Or are they movie stars or celebrities who never seem to age

Mr WONKA was very happy to pay for the shopping spree

Although he paid even more than he paid for his own house
They are now going to meet Mr President and have afternoon tea
He will welcome them with a red carpet in front of the White House

When they approached the helicopter, the pilot looked at the grandmas and asked the rest, "Did you lose the glandmas? These two ladies are …....?" He could hardly recognize the two ladies who were actually the two grandmas clothed in beautiful and elegant dresses.

Once they were all in the helicopter, the pilot spoke into the radio to give notification that they were running late according to the schedule but he would pick up the speed once they were in the air. The engine roared and the propellers started to spin and the helicopter rose slowly into the sky from the top of the shopping mall. It quickly became a small black dot and then totally disappeared in the blue sky.

8 The Welcome Ceremony on the North Lawn

The north lawn of the White House was the President's front yard. It was bordered on the north by Pennsylvania Avenue with a wide view of the mansion, and was screened by dense plantings on the east from East Executive Drive and the Treasury Building, and on the west from West Executive Drive and the Old Executive Office Building. Because it was bordered by Pennsylvania Avenue, the White House's official street address, the North Lawn was sometimes described as the front lawn. It had many old trees and other plantings, some of which dated back nearly the full two hundred years of the White House's existence.

A semicircular driveway ran from the northwest gate through the North Portico, sweeping back to Pennsylvania Avenue through the northeast gate. A circular pool with fountain was centered on the north portico of the White House.

In the time of President Tyler, the acclaimed author Charles Dickens wrote of his visit, *"The President's mansion is more like an English clubhouse, both within and without, than any other kind of establishment with which I can compare it. The ornamental ground about it has been laid out in garden walks; they are pretty, and agreeable to the eye; though they have that uncomfortable air of having been made yesterday, which is far from favourable to the display of such beauties."*

Public tours, which began on East Executive Drive, exited through the North Portico, and visitors exited from the northeast gate. Visiting heads of state entered the White House grounds, and were officially welcomed here prior to a state dinner. This was exactly what would happen to our heroes today. They would be welcomed by the President on the north lawn before they had a dinner with him.

The President of the United States was standing on the lawn of the White House. He was surrounded by all the most important people in the country. They were wearing their best clothes and there was an air of tremendous excitement everywhere. The President himself was gazing anxiously at the sky. He was searching for the helicopter which was due to arrive at any minute. This helicopter, as everyone knew, was bringing to the White House the eight brave astronauts who only about ten hours before had rescued an American spaceship when it was attacked by a swarm or Vermicious Knids.

So, standing on the lawn were: The President of the United States, Lancelot R Gilligrass, one of the most powerful men on earth. The Vice-President, Miss Tibbs, a gigantic and fearsome lady of eighty-nine who had been the President's nanny when he was small. Mrs Taubsypass, the President's famous cat. Then we had the President's Inner Cabinet. This consisted of five men. They were the President's closest advisers and they were all immensely powerful. Together with the President and Vice-President, these five men ran the country. They were: The Chief of the Army: General Horsebrass, who was wearing so many medal-ribbons they covered not only the front and back of his tunic but ran all the way down his pants as well. The Chief of the Navy, Admiral Tarbuncle, who was **all at sea on land**. The chief of the Air Force, Admiral Osborne, who always walked past people with his nose **in the air**. The Director of Sewage and Garbage Disposal, the Honourable I. M. Ponky, who was standing all by himself because nobody wanted to come too close to him, even downwind. The Director of Public Relations and Bamboozlement, Wilbur G Pocus, known as Hocus to his friends. The coordinator of Hi-Fi and Hearing Aids, Mr. Bugsy Tape, who was hiding in a hollow tree and recording every word that was spoken on the White House lawn. The sword swallower from Afghanistan, who was the President's best friend, was also there. There were lots of other famous and important people there, but there wasn't room to mention them all.

A huge crowd of correspondents, for newspaper and television news, were standing on the North Lawn with the North Portico as a backdrop. They, together with other government officials and millions of television audience, were waiting anxiously for the arrival of the helicopter.

Finally, the noise of the helicopter could be heard from far far away. All the people standing outside the White House became a little agitated and everyone started to look up. Initially the helicopter appeared in the sky like a dragonfly and its size was increasing by every second. By the time the President and his men and all the other important people were in their positions, it was hovering not very high over the White House and started to descend slowly. The noise became much bigger and the wind became much stronger and finally it landed lightly and softly on the ground not far from the White House.

People were cheering and applauding as the eight national heroes walked out of the helicopter with their arms linked again. The President, the Vice President and the Inner Cabinet shook hands warmly with each of them. Once the greeting and the handshaking was finished and everyone was in position, the President commenced the welcome ceremony with his speech.

"OUR DEAR *LATE* MR WILLY WONKA ET AL. SORRY, I MEANT OUR DEAR BELATED MR WILLY WONKA ET AL.

TODAY, THE ENTIRE NATION, INDEED THE WHOLE WORLD IS REJOICING AT THE SAFE RETURN OF OUR TRANSPORT CAPSULE FROM SPACE WITH 136 SOULS ON BOARD. HAD IT NOT BEEN FOR THE HELP THEY RECEIVED FROM AN UNKNOWN SPACESHIP, THESE 136 PEOPLE WOULD NEVER HAVE COME BACK. IT HAS BEEN REPORTED TO ME THAT THE COURAGE SHOWN BY THE EIGHT ASTRONAUTS ABOARD THIS UNKNOWN SPACESHIP WAS EXTRAORDINARY. OUR RADAR STATIONS, BY TRACKING THIS SPACESHIP ON ITS RETURN TO EARTH HAVE DISCOVERED THAT IT SPLASHED DOWN IN A PLACE KNOWN AS WONKA'S CHOCOLATE FACTORY. THAT, MR WILLY WONKA ET AL., IS WHY A LETTER WAS DELIVERED TO YOU TO INVITE YOU TO COME AND STAY IN THE WHITE HOUSE FOR A FEW DAYS AS MY HONOURED GUESTS."

While the crowd cheered and applauded again, Charlie said to Mr WONKA, "Wasn't Mr President reading the same letter that was delivered to you?"

"Yes, he was, basically." said Mr WONKA. "Probably his secretary didn't have enough time to write another speech for him."

The president's voice resonated again in the powerful loudspeakers, "We will now pin medals for bravery upon all eight of these gallant fliers." The President pinned platinum medals for all of them one by one.

When it came to the grandparents, Mr WONKA had to introduce them to Mr President one by one. After shaking the hands of Grandpa Joe and Grandma Josephine as Mr Bucket's parents, Mr WONKA introduced Grandpa George and Grandma Georgina as the in-laws.

Grandma Georgina, who was still in the mood of joking said, "Do you know the difference between in-laws and outlaws? **Outlaws are always wanted while in-laws are not.**"

With the platinum medal pinned on his jacket, Mr WONKA responded to Mr President's speech. At the conclusion of his speech, he said, "We are very delighted and grateful indeed to be invited by Mr President to stay in the White House for a few days as his honoured guests. I have no doubt that if anyone else had been in the great glass elevator, he would have done the same thing. So, please forget about the past, as we cannot change it. Forget about the future, as we cannot predict it. And forget about the **present**, as I forgot to bring you one, Mr President."

"But did you bring a few WONKA fudgemallow delights as my presents as requested in the letter?" Mr President asked eagerly for fear that Mr WONKA really forgot to bring them.

"Yes, of course," said Mr WONKA with a grin. "In fact, not just a few, but enough for everyone who will be present at the dinner tonight." Mr WONKA pointed at the two containers which had already been unloaded from the helicopter.

"That's great! Thank you for your present." The President said. "We will consume them as desserts for our dinner. Can we have them sent to the kitchen, please?"

He then turned to the crowd, "Any questions you wish to ask our heroes, please keep them for the press conference to be held prior to the dinner tonight."

"I have just one simple question not for our heroes but for you, Mr President if I may ask." A very young correspondent raised his hand.

The President nodded and the young man proceeded with his question, "Why was the building called the White House? Was it called the White House because it was painted white or had it already been named White House even before it was constructed and then painted white?"

"Good question." said the President, scratching his head and searching for the right answer. "We all know there was Red Square in Russia, Yellow River in China, Blue Mountains in Australia, Greenland near Arctic, Black Sea in Eurasia, etc, etc, but there was nothing white." He paused, still searching for a better answer. "But the real reason why we named it White House is that people always tend to think politicians are liars. We just want those who call us liars to know that all the lies which originate from the White House are **white lies**. I hope that answers your query, young man."

The President was very pleased with his answer. He then turned joyfully to our heroes, "Rooms have been carefully selected and prepared for you already. Please go and have a rest. You will have the press conference to attend soon. I will see you all at dinner which will start at 7pm."

9 In the Guest Rooms

Participants of the Overnight Guest Program were usually allowed entry via the prestigious West Wing Entrance at 19:00, but as the heroes were invited by the President as special guests, the Secret Service assisted them to find their rooms straight after the welcome ceremony. They were informed that they would have unprecedented guest access to all areas of the White House. They were also informed that after they settled in, they were free to roam the halls for a self-guided tour with detailed maps provided for their convenience. They were to wear the "SG" badges at all times, which would identify them as Special Guests with Level-5 access. In addition, they were informed that certain areas of the White House would require knowledge of a daily access password. They would receive the password upon check-in and they needed to make sure to memorize it.

What's more, as participants of the Overnight Guest Program, they could

- have commemorative photos taken by Official White House Photographer
- use the library, bowling alley, movie theatre, swimming pool, and basketball court
- have breakfast in the family dining room
- have a self-guided tour throughout the White House complex. Photos allowed, but no videos.

As a bonus, they could have access to the underground tunnels, hidden staircases, etc. except the First Family's bedrooms.

Charlie thought the underground tunnels and the hidden staircases were the places he was really interested in. He was really curious to find out what was happening down there.

As one of the First Ladies said about the White House: *"I hope we've done a good job of bringing even more people to this place — people who never thought they were connected to this history. Just increasing that curiosity that this White House is yours, everyone's. It doesn't belong to a set of special people who have access and privilege. It's everyone's house, at every age. So come, use this place, walk in the doors. Feel like it's your museum."*

All the luxurious bedrooms were furnished with fine antiques and historic Presidential beds. Thick white towels and Aveda hair products were provided.

Five spacious bedrooms had been carefully selected and set aside for our heroes. One for Mr WONKA, one for Charlie, one for Mr and Mrs Bucket, one for Grandpa Joe and Grandma Josephine and one for

Grandpa George and Grandma Georgina. The grandparents were so surprised and thrilled when we saw their bedrooms.

The grandparents got the Queen's bedrooms, which were named for the many royal guests including Queen Elizabeth II of the United Kingdom, Queen Sonja of Norway, and Queen Sofía of Spain. These richly decorated rooms were furnished in the Federal Style evoking an early-19th-century New England bedroom featuring the bed of Andrew Jackson.

The armchairs, the beds and the hanging drapery silks were all Scalamandré exclusives, decorated with period artwork and colored prints worthy of the most discerning collector. Each room also had a sitting area with full-size sofas and chairs, a writing desk, and inlaid armoires. Great view of the North Lawn! Bath had Jacuzzi tub and shower with separate dressing area.

Mr WONKA, Charlie and the Buckets got the Lincoln Bedrooms, which were artfully restored incorporating Lincoln period details such as window cornices and mantel. The centerpiece of the room was the 8-foot by 6-foot Rosewood Lincoln bed.

The gilded carved bed canopy was in the shape of a crown with flowing yards of regal purple satin over white lace trailing to the floor. The bed hanging satin, drapery silk, tassels and tiebacks were also Scalamandré exclusives. The furniture used by the Lincoln Administration included the sofa and three matching chairs, two slipper chairs, and four of Lincoln's Cabinet chairs.

Guests staying in the Lincoln Bedroom would have the use of the Lincoln bathroom, installed during the Truman presidency, with pale green opaque glass tiles and a mirrored dome ceiling light. The spacious tub had an elegant sandblasted etching of a Presidential eagle.

"Good heavens! This giant bed can accommodate 10 people!" Grandpa Joe screamed.

"The bathroom is as big as our Town Hall!" Grandma Josephine cried.

"The walk-in-robe is a decent dressing room!" Grandpa George yelled.

"There is even a courtyard off the French sliding doors!" Grandma Georgina shrieked.

While the grandparents kept on admiring their bedrooms, the Buckets unpacked their luggage for their parents as well as for themselves.

After Mr WONKA had left his luggage in his room, he came to see Charlie immediately. "What shall we do with the fudgemallow delights now?"

Charlie didn't look worried at all, "What do you mean?"

"The pilot took the fudgemallow delights in the helicopter. He shouldn't have done that before the President."

"What shall we do then?" Charlie looked calm and collected.

"I shouldn't and certainly don't want to say it. We have no any other way but to get rid of him. The scripture reads, *'Behold the Lord sayeth the wicked to bring forth his righteous purposes. It is better that one man should perish than that a nation should dwindle and perish in unbelief.'*

"I know that verse. But that's the wrong application of the scripture, I'm afraid." Charlie snapped.

"Now you have got the magic power as well, can you order him, as you ordered him to land on the top of the shopping mall, to commit suicide for the world so that our plan will not go wrong?"

"But that's not the right thing to do, either." Charlie replied.

"Come, Charlie, come with me. Hurry up." He dragged Charlie out of the bedroom.

"Why?" asked Charlie, who was still admiring the magnificent room just like his grandparents. "Where are we going?"

"Just come with me. Hurry up. I will tell you on the way" Mr WONKA took hold of Charlie's arm and pulled him forward.

Once they were out walking quietly in the long corridor towards the kitchen, Mr WONKA said, "We are going to the kitchen. We must either destroy or take the fudgemallow delights back before it is too late. Otherwise, the President and his men will take them as desserts at the banquet tonight."

"But they were meant to be gifts for the President and his men and they have already been sent to the kitchen."

"That's why we should go and destroy or steal the two containers now and ......" Before Mr WONKA could finish his sentence, the two of them were already right outside the kitchen, so he had to stop talking.

The kitchen door was ajar and to their dismay, as they could see not far away from the door, the two containers had already been opened and on the huge benchtop, there were about 100 dessert plates each containing a WONKA fudgemallow delight. Obviously, they had already been set up as part of the desserts.

"Oh, my goodness." Mr WONKA exclaimed, looking at the fudgemallow delights and then at Charlie "We are too late. We cannot destroy or steal them anymore. Let's go back now and see what else we can do."

When they came back from the kitchen, Mr WONKA said to Charlie, "We cannot do anything now. It's too late. There's nothing we can do

Starting from tomorrow, in fact, after the banquet tonight, the pilot will have total control of the President. He will be the real President of the country and the whole world will be thrown into a chaos."

Charlie still looked calm and collected as if that was not a serious problem at all. He gave out a chuckle and said, "I am not worried about that at all."

"What?" Mr WONKA cried. "Think of this. The pilot will be the boss of the President and he will be in control of all the nuclear weapons and the missiles powerful and *tramenastic* enough to destroy the earth more than ten times."

"Think of this." Charlie said to Mr WONKA in the same way. "True, the pilot is the boss of the President, but who is the boss of the pilot? His mind is controlled by us now, not by himself. We can easily order him not to control the President."

"But we cannot constantly give orders to him. Day and night, I mean." Mr WONKA looked really worried.

"Don't worry, Mr WONKA." Charlie said calmly. "First, I think the pilot will retire very soon. That was what he told me when I said goodbye to him before I got off the helicopter. Second and more importantly, he is just a pilot. You know the first and foremost duty of a soldier is to be obedient. He will never think of giving orders to or controlling the President unless he and his wife swap their roles, which is highly impossible in our case."

"I never thought of that. What would we do without you? You mean we can just go and relax and enjoy the banquet tonight?" Mr WONKA sighed with relief.

"Yes, basically. But we need to make sure that the President takes it first." Charlie replied.

"What if the kitchen staff take it first?" Mr WONKA started to worry again.

"Don't worry, Mr WONKA. You're worrying too much these days." Charlie said. "They are prohibited to eat any food first although a chemical test might be conducted if the food is not sourced from their own garden or nominated suppliers. That's the rule in the kitchen of the White House. They may only eat the leftovers if any. I learnt their rules in an article in the newspaper, which I think are true and make sense."

"Ok. But how can we make sure that the President takes the fudgemallow delights first?" Mr WONKA started to look worried once more.

"We will have to wait and see." Charlie said. "For now, let's unpack our luggage, have a shower and get changed for the press conference."

10 The Press Conference

The press conference was held just before the welcome banquet in the James S. Brady Press Briefing Room which was a small theatre in the West Wing of the White House where the White House Press Secretary gave briefings to the news media and the President of the United States sometimes addressed the press and the nation. It was located between the workspace assigned to the White House press corps and the office of the Press Secretary.

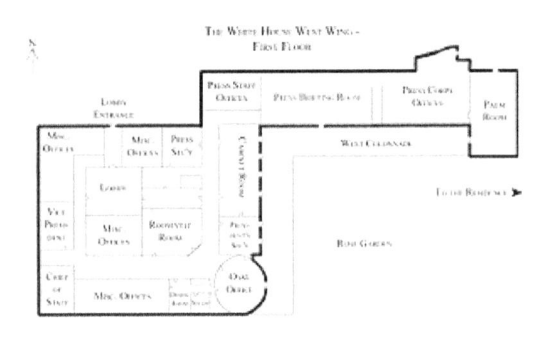

There was a seven row seating chart for the Room and journalists and correspondents from TV and radio stations, newspaper and the forty-nine magazines, such as Reuters, Fox News, Washington Post, Wall Street Journal, New York Times, etc. had already filled the seats long before the heroes arrived.

PODIUM

NBC	Fox News	CBS News	Associated Press	ABC News	Reuters	CNN
Wall Street Journal	CBS Radio	Bloomberg	NPR	Washington Post	New York Times	Associated Press Radio
AFP	USA Today	McClatchy	American Urban Radio Networks	POLITICO	Tribune	ABC Radio
Foreign Pool	MSNBC	Washington Times	The Hill	Fox News Radio	Voice of America	National Journal
Bloomberg BNA	TIME	New York Daily News	Hearst, S.F. Chronicle, Baltimore Sun	New York Post	Real Clear Politics	Chicago Sun-Times, Al Jazeera
Washington Examiner	Yahoo! News	Salem Radio Network	Media News Group, The Daily Beast	Christian Science Monitor	Sirius XM	Dow Jones
Talk Radio News Service	Dallas Morning News	Roll Call	CBN News	BBC, The Boston Globe	Scripps, BuzzFeed	Financial Times, The Guardian

The press conference was, as usual, quite boring or interesting as some people saw it.

Charlie was still a bit nervous when he entered the room although he had the experience of being surrounded and bombarded by a huge crowd of reporters when he won the chocolate bar with the golden ticket. "I don't know what to say and how to respond to the reporters."

"Don't worry too much." said Mr WONKA. "Just remember the five ups. **Stand up, walk up, speak up, wind up and then shut up.**"

The press conference commenced right on the dot with a welcome speech by President Lancelot R. Gilligrass. He started the ball rolling by saying, "My speech today will be like a mini-skirt. Long enough to cover the essentials but short enough to hold your attention." He expressed his gratitude to the eight national heroes again and then made a very detailed recount of the event. There was nothing substantial to announce to the public yet so the press conference was merely an opportunity for the reporters to ask questions with regard to the event and some other issues that intrigued them.

The journalists were very satisfied with the recount presented by the President and they either recorded it or took detailed notes on their mobile devices. None of them asked for more details about the event per se. Instead, they were more interested in the feelings and emotions and well beings of the heroes.

The following was an incomplete and *puccInitve* record of the questions asked by the journalists and the answers provided by our heroes. The names of the journalists and their respective workplaces had been left out while the names of our heroes had been retained. The questions were not in chronological order as listed below but that really didn't matter.

Journalist A: "How would you reflect upon your past and think of your future?"

Mrs Bucket: "My grammar teacher who taught us aspects and tenses of English once said, 'Past is tense, the future perfect.' I believe that is the most applicable answer to your question, gentleman."

Journalist B: "Have you ever showed your intelligence like that before?"

Mr WONKA: "Intelligence is like your underwear. It is important that you have it, but not necessary that you show it off. However, even if you don't show it off, I know, as a newspaper reporter, you wear news briefs."

Journalist C: "How would you describe your relationship with your grandson?"

Grandma Georgina: "Somewhere an elderly lady reads a book on how to use the internet, while a young boy googles 'how to read a book'".

Journalist D: "What do you do in your spare time?"

Grandma Josephine: "Most people have got Facebook. I just face a book."

Journalist E: "And you, Grandpa Joe. What do you do in your spare time?"

Grandpa Joe: "I sometimes play Uno with Charlie. However, I can never play Uno with Mexicans because they would steal all the **green cards**."

Journalist F: "At your age, what do you think you still want to achieve?"

Grandpa Joe: "To me age is not important unless I am wine or cheese. In fact, age is an issue of mind over matter. If you don't mind, it doesn't matter. Hahahaha."

Journalist G: "What do you think is the key to success?"

Mr Bucket: "Whenever I find the key to success, someone changes the lock."

Journalist H: "Do you think you are a successful man?"

Mr Bucket: "A successful man is one who makes more money than his wife can spend. A successful woman is one who can find such a man."

Grandma Josephine added, "Behind every successful man is his woman. Behind the fall of a successful man is usually another woman.

Journalist I: "I know you were going to say that."

Mrs Bucket: "If you say 'I knew you were going to say that' enough, you can start billing people for psychic readings."

Journalist J: "Why are you all wearing sunglasses today?"

Charlie: "We are wearing sunglasses today not because of your dazzling flashlights, but because you are all too **bright**!"

"Ladies and gentlemen," interrupted the President, "I am sure you have a million more questions to ask, but I am afraid our heroes need to retreat to get ready for the welcome banquet tonight. Thank you for attending this special press conference, which we will now bring to a close."

While the press conference was a great success, Mr WONKA was still thinking how the President could be the first one to take the fudgemallow delights at the welcome banquet tonight.

11 The Welcome Banquet

The State Dining Room was the larger of the two dining rooms on the State Floor of the Executive Residence of the White House, the home of the President of the United States in Washington, D.C. It was used for receptions, luncheons, larger formal dinners, and state dinners for visiting heads of state on state visits. The room seated 140 and measured approximately 48 by 36 feet (or 15 by 11 metres).

Originally office space, the State Dining Room received its name during the presidency of James Monroe, at which time it was first extensively furnished. The room was refurbished during several administrations in the early to mid 1800s, and gasified in 1853. Doors were cut through the west wall in 1877. The State Dining Room underwent a major expansion and renovation in 1902, transforming it from a Victorian dining room into a "baronial" dining hall of the early 19th century - complete with stuffed animal heads on the walls and dark oak panelling. The room stayed in this form until the White House's complete reconstruction in 1952.

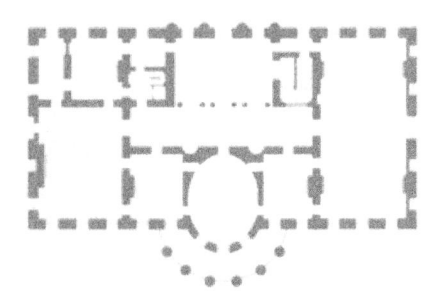

The 1952 rebuilding of the White House retained much of the 1902 renovation, although much of the "baronial" furnishings were removed and the walls were painted celadon green. Another major refurbishment from 1961 to 1963 changed the room even further, more closely approximating an Empire style room with elements from a wide range of other periods. Incremental changes to the room were made throughout the 1970s and 1980s, with major refurbishments of the furnishings in 1998 and 2015.

The heroes and the President arrived almost at the same time. All the 140 seats were now filled by the Inner Cabinet, ministers, heads of state and other VIPs who were already there, including the Vice President Miss Elvira TIBBS, the Chief of the Army, Navy and Airforce, members of the congress, the Sword Swallower, the Chief interpreter, and Governors of every state.

Fortunately, the Chief of the Army, Navy and Airforce were at the same main table with the President, the Vice President and the eight heroes.

The beautifully designed and printed menu revealed it was a five course dinner with fudgemallow delights as the dessert.

MENU

CANAPÉ

SMOKED BACON WRAPPED APRICOTS ROASTED IN HONEY, MUSTARD & SOY

STARTER

MUSSELS COOKED IN DEVON CIDER WITH CREAM, BACON & HOT CRUSTY BREAD

MAIN COURSE

BRITISH GRASS FED 8OZ FILLET STEAK, CRISPY GARLIC ROAST POTATOES, GREEN BEANS & CREAMY DIJON SAUCE

DESSERT

FUDGEMALLOW DELIGHTS WITH CINNAMON CREAM & FRESH ORANGE

CHEESE

CHEF'S FAVORITE CHEESES (MIN 4 TYPES) WITH FRESH FRUIT, HOMEMADE CHUTNEY & OATCAKE/CRACKER SELECTION

The noise level subdued quickly when the President and the eight heroes entered the dining hall. As soon as they were guided to their table and seated, the President stood up. Trying to look at everyone in the enormous dining room, the President announced that the banquet could commence without any more formal speeches to be delivered as they already had the welcome ceremony and the press conference. People could just enjoy the food and talk among themselves to catch up with each other. However, he said he would propose a toast during the course of the banquet.

"Thank you again for the courageous act." The President said and while picking up his canopy, he turned to Charlie, "Charlie, what a brave and smart boy you are! As one of the most powerful people in the world, I would like to grant you three wishes."

"My wishes have already come true," Charlie replied, knowing the President would still grant him more wishes. "I told Mr WONKA the same thing. I have got the chocolate bar with the gold ticket. I have visited the chocolate factory. I have seen all the secrets and magic of the factory and I have been given enough chocolates and sweets that will last me for the rest of my life. What else should I wish for?"

"Are you sure you don't have any more wishes?" The President asked the same question as Mr WONKA did. "Is there anything else I can do for you?"

"If you really want me to have more wishes, then I just wish I could share and enjoy all the chocolates and sweets with my family in peace. And that we could all love one another." Charlie gave the same answer as he did to Mr WONKA without any hesitation.

The President put down the canape he was trying to put into his mouth, "That's an excellent idea. A very mature idea indeed, Charlie. But how can I do it? I am afraid even my think tank wouldn't know how I can achieve this."

"You will have to destroy all your missiles, chemical and nuclear weapons, if I may say so. I don't think it is right to possess all those weapons." Charlie said boldly and straightforwardly.

"Well," the President picked up the canopy from his plate again and put it into his mouth, "War is not about who is right, but who is **left**."

Charlie looked at Mr WONKA who gave him a wink as if saying, "Told you! He would not change his mind at all! He would not change a thing!"

The waiters and the waitresses started to serve the starters and Mr WONKA was worried how the President could be the first one to take the fudgemallow delights at the banquet. He thought he should somehow mention the fudgemallow delights well before they were served as desserts.

"You know what, Mr President?" Mr WONKA could not afford not to mention the fudgemallow delights. "When I was a little kid, we always had our desserts first because everyone in the family had a sweet tooth."

"Right," the President said. "I almost forget that we will have your fudgemallow delights for desserts tonight. Whenever I feel stressed, I just read the word **stressed** back to front."

"**Stressed** back to front..." Admiral Tarbuncle repeated. "That means **desserts**." He then turned to General Horsebrass and Admiral Osborne, "We should do the same when we are stressed."

When you're stressed, you eat chocolate and sweets. *you know why*??

Because "stressed" spellled backwards is "Desserts"

"That's just one of my ways to relieve my stress." The President said. "Really wish I could have a bite right now just like Mr WONKA's family having desserts at the beginning of the dinner. But I'm afraid we will have to wait until we are served."

Charlie said, "Yes, Mr President, you should have a taste of them now before the main courses are served."

"But Charlie," Mr WONKA said, "I don't think it is courteous and appropriate to fetch some fudgemallow delights from the kitchen now."

"Voila!" Charlie cried out, holding a fudgemallow delight in his right hand. "I've got one here, Mr President. Would you like to try it now?"

Mr WONKA was staring at Charlie with his mouth open, totally speechless.

"Of course. I would love to." The President took it from Charlie and put it in his mouth. "Mm… As good as ever." He finished eating it in no time.

The waiters and the waitresses started to serve the main courses. Grandpa Joe was a bit surprised to see that General Horsebrass's plate only had roast potatoes and green beans so he called out to one of the waiters, "Excuse me, but I think you missed the steak for General Horsebrass."

Before the waiter tried to explain, General Horsebrass said, "He is right. It's not a **missteak**. I am a vegetarian. That's why my last name has a horse in it and rhymes with grass. Haha. I am a vegetarian not because I love animals but because I hate vegetables. Hahahaha."

Grandma Josephine said, "I used to eat a lot of natural foods until I learned that most people die of natural causes."

Grandpa George had been very quiet all the time, but upon hearing General Horsebrass and Grandma Josephine's remarks, he said, "I eat a lot of food with preservatives now because I want to **preserve** my age."

Mrs Bucket, who was a woman of few words just like her dad, said, "I have abstained from eating nuts because my doctor always tells me 'You are what you eat'. I thought if I ate nuts, then I would be **nuts**." Everyone burst out laughing.

YOU ARE WHAT

YOU EAT

The atmosphere was amicable and enjoyable. The band was performing live music softly in the corner of the dining room. The President said, "I have requested some well known and successful musicians from different states to perform for us on this special occasion."

Admiral Osborne, who was very musical with the trumpet, added with a smile, "I am not **blowing my own trumpet**, but I think the **key** to the success of all musicians of **note** is their ability to stay **composed** while performing at a level that can't be **beat**."

After the music stopped for the next one, the President took the opportunity to stand up with his wine glass in his hand, "Ladies and gentlemen! I now propose a toast for our eight brave heroes, who are also my special guests. I wish to express my gratitude to them once again for the courage and valiance they displayed. We will be infinitely indebted to them. Cheers!"

"Cheers!" everybody echoed.

The President then went to different tables to talk to other important people.

"Charlie," Mr WONKA moved away to sit next to Charlie now that the President's seat was vacant. He spoke to Charlie in a voice that could only be heard by the two of them. "The desserts will be served very soon. Our plan was to have the President and then the chiefs to have the fudgemallow delights first. Do you have more of them to offer to the chiefs now?"

"No," Charlie replied straight away.

"Then, how can we get the chiefs to have the fudgemallow delights first? I know our table will be served with desserts first, but it won't take long for the other tables to get theirs and some of the guests might have their desserts first before the chiefs do. Unlike the pilot whom we can probably ignore, they are the most powerful bunch of people in the country and they can have their own opinions on certain things. It's going to be messy again."

"Well, why don't you …" Charlie whispered into Mr WONKA's ear.

"Charlie, what would we do without you?", Mr WONKA exclaimed in a subdued voice.

The music went on. The President was still busy talking to people. And the waiters and waitresses started to place desserts on the main table.

There was no moment to lose. Mr WONKA stood up and made a quick announcement with a loud voice that everybody could hear clearly in spite of the live music in the background. "Ladies and gentlemen! On behalf of Charlie, his parents and his grandparents, I would like to thank Mr President for inviting us as his special guests to spend a few days in the White House and to have dinner with him and his officials. I propose a toast for him and his officials for the great work that they do for the country. Cheers!"

"Cheers!" everybody echoed again.

Mr WONKA continued, "For those who attended the welcome ceremony this afternoon, you will know that fudgemallow delights will be served as desserts tonight. I brought those fudgemallow delights for Mr President as our special gifts. I suggest that we all wait until Mr President takes them first to show our respect and reverence."

Once everyone at the main table had received the desserts, Mr WONKA said to the chiefs, "You may start having your desserts now."

"But don't we have to wait until Mr President returns to our table to have his first?" The Chief of the Navy, Admiral Tarbuncle, asked.

"No." Mr WONKA said, "Remember Charlie brought a few of them for him and he had a taste of them before the main course? He is having a good time talking to the people over there. So please do start without him. Please! I said those words simply because of the formality, just to make him happy."

The chiefs couldn't wait for the desserts and they pounced on them and devoured them like hungry wolves devouring their prey, totally ignoring their manners.

The President was still talking to other people, having a good time. He then saw the Chief Interpreter sitting at a table not far away from the main table. The Chief Interpreter didn't notice that the President was approaching him as he was busy receiving and sending his messages as usual. The President walked up to him and chuckled, "Well, what a message! **What a mess age**! You may just relax and enjoy your dinner tonight. Our heroes are not aliens as we thought and they don't speak the alien language…..."

Before he could say anything more to the Chief Interpreter, one of the waiters came up to the President and said, "Excuse me, Mr President. If you could please return to your table to have your desserts so that all your cabinet and other guests may have the **delight** to have the delights as well."

"Sorry, but I have been busy chatting and talking." The President said. "Are they all waiting for me to return to my table? Actually I had mine well before the main course. Anyway, I will go back to my table now." He returned to his table swiftly and made a quick announcement to all the guests, "Thank you to Mr WONKA for bringing us the delicious desserts. Now let's enjoy our desserts." After that, he walked away from his table to resume his talk with the Chief Interpreter.

Once he was gone, Mr WONKA whispered to Charlie again. "Charlie, I'm afraid you have another job to do."

"What job are you talking about?" Charlie asked. "We have successfully fulfilled our tasks already."

"What about the remaining fudgemallow delights in the kitchen? It will be really messy if the chefs take them home to feed their families or dogs."

"Good thinking, Mr WONKA." Charlie said. "I will go to the kitchen right now to get them."

"Will they let you take them?" Asked Mr WONKA." Once they are in the kitchen, they belong to the White House."

"But they are, or were, ours." Charlie replied. "And we brought them to the White House. Don't worry. They will still be ours."

Charlie headed towards the kitchen straight away. When he got there, he saw one of the chefs starting to pack up the remaining fudgemallow delights. He knocked on the door politely, "Excuse me and sorry to intrude. I know you have the right to take the fudgemallow delights home to feed your dogs or do whatever you wish with them but I would like to take them all and give them to Mr President. We brought those especially for Mr President because someone kept on stealing them from his drawer."

"Fair enough." said the chef who handed them back to Charlie with some reluctance and *unwaidiness*.

When Charlie came back to the table, the President was talking on his phone. When he finished, he said to the heroes, "I am sorry but I have to go to deal with a matter. Please enjoy the rest of the night. As I said, as my special guests and national heroes, you are welcome to stay as long as you wish. Have a nice evening!"

"Thank you, Mr President." All the eight heroes replied almost at the same time.

The dinner and the music went on but the heroes especially the grandparents felt extremely exhausted after the flight, the shopping spree, the welcome ceremony and the press conference so they had to excuse themselves and left early.

When they were making their way back to their bedrooms, Mr WONKA couldn't help asking Charlie, "How did you get the fudgemallow delights for the President?"

"I have learnt to carry a spare one in my **spare** time. Otherwise, I will not be **spared**. Haha."

"What would we do without you, Charlie? We need some good sleep tonight." Mr WONKA said as they were approaching their respective bedrooms. "Good night!"

As soon as Charlie entered his bedroom, he threw himself on to the bed, but he couldn't fall asleep immediately. Something was puzzling him. Something strange. Something weird. Something *utoustatipalic*. Something that was not quite right. What was that? He thought and thought and then it suddenly dawned on him that it was the President's voice. He knew his voice quite well because he had heard his speeches several times on TV before, and he spoke to them while they were in the Space Hotel only a few days ago. The President's voice he heard at the welcome ceremony and at the dinner was different in that it sounded as if he had a mild cold and there was an almost unnoticeable slight delay in all his responses. Maybe there really WAS something weird. Maybe that was his wrong impression and feeling. He tried to think hard but felt too tired to think any more and fell into deep sleep.

12 Second day in the White House

It was almost ten o'clock when the heroes woke up although the grandparents woke up a little earlier. They must have been exhausted after a long day yesterday.

After a sumptuous breakfast in the family room, which was much better than any Christmas dinner for the Buckets family, they were ready to have a self guided tour in the White House with detailed maps provided for their convenience as promised.

They all decided to take their time for a walk around the building first and when they came out of the building, they found themselves in front of the north front of the building, the principal façade of the White House, which was of three floors and eleven bays. The ground floor was hidden by a raised carriage ramp and parapet, thus the façade appeared to be of two floors. The central three bays were behind a prostyle portico (this was a later addition to the house, built circa 1830) serving, thanks to the carriage ramp, as a porte cochere. The windows of the four bays flanking the portico, at first-floor level, had alternating pointed and segmented pediments, while at second-floor level the pediments were flat. The principal entrance at the center of the Cportico was surmounted by alunette fanlight. Above the entrance was a sculpted floral festoon. The roofline was hidden by a balustradedparapet.

They kept on looking and marvelling at the building while slowly moving to the mansion's southern façade, which was a combination of the Palladian and neoclassical styles of architecture. It was of three floors, all visible. The ground floor was rusticated in the Palladian fashion. At the center of the façade was a neoclassical projecting bow of three bays. The bow was flanked by five bays, the windows of which, as on the north façade, had alternating segmented and pointed pediments at first-floor level. The bow had a ground floor double staircase leading to an Ionic colonnaded loggia (with the Truman Balcony at second-floor level), known as the south portico. The more modern third floor was hidden by a balustraded parapet and played no part in the composition of the façade.

As soon as they entered the building to have a look at the inside, they could hear the voice of a tourist guide who was introducing the building to a group of tourists, "...... The modern-day White House complex includes the Executive Residence, West Wing, East Wing, the Eisenhower Executive Office Building -- the former State Department, which now houses offices for the President's staff and the Vice President -- and Blair House, a guest residence. The Executive Residence is made up of six storeys -- the Ground Floor, State Floor, Second Floor, and Third Floor, as well as a two-storey basement."

The guide took out his water bottle, had a drink, and continued his introduction. "Today the group of buildings housing the presidency is known as the White House Complex. It includes the central Executive Residence flanked by the East Wing and West Wing. The Chief Usher coordinates day to day household operations. The White House includes: six storeys and 55,000 ft² (5,100 m²) of floor space, 132 rooms and 35 bathrooms, 412 doors, 147 windows, twenty-eight fireplaces, eight staircases, three elevators, five full-time chefs, a tennis court, a (single-lane) bowling alley (officially called the Harry S. Truman Bowling Alley), a movie theater (officially called the White House Family Theater), a jogging track, a swimming pool, and a putting green. It receives up to 30,000 visitors each week."

Grandma Georgina said, "Sorry, we don't belong to your group but we couldn't help overhearing it. That's a splendid introduction of the White House. Thank you." She then turned around and said to the others, "Shall we follow them around the building?"

"No, we can't grandma." Charlie said. "This is paid service for the tourist group. We are meant to take our own self guided tour."

"Ok, I understand." Grandma Georgina said. "Just wait till the tourist guide finishes his next comment and I will be ready to leave them and join you."

The tourist guide obviously heard what Grandma said and gave her a smile. He then went on with his introduction, "On Saturday, 1 November, 1800, John Adams became the first president to take residence in the building. During Adam's second day in the house, he wrote a letter to his wife, Abigail, containing a prayer for the house. Adams wrote,

"I pray Heaven to bestow the best of blessings on this House, and all that shall hereafter inhabit it. May none but honest and wise men ever rule under this roof."

Grandma Georgina asked the guide, "When I was a child, I always wondered why people would say **Amen** but not **Awomen** at the end of a prayer. Do you know why?" She obviously didn't want to leave the group.

"Sorry, I don't have a clue." The guide replied.

Grandma Georgina laughed and said, "I think because in the church, you always sing **hymn**, not **her**. By the way, do you know in what **state** John Adams was born?"

"Sorry, I have no idea." The guide shook his head again.

"Haha," Grandma Georgina grinned again, "Naked and screaming like the rest of us." She then said, "Thank you for your marvellous introduction. I won't harass you anymore." Then she waved to the whole group, "Have a good day!"

Grandma Georgina joined the rest of the family and they continued their way to explore the rest of the White House. With the grandparents moving slowly, it took them almost an hour and a half to complete their self guided tour above the ground.

As they were ready to visit the basement, the President walked past and asked them if they had a good sleep and enjoyed their self guided tour. He said he had been called away to deal with an emergency and should be back late in the afternoon.

Grandpa George already looked very tired and said, "That's enough for me. I need a rest now. If I don't get a **break**, I will surely **break** down."

The other three grandparents also felt tired and **vilatumetical** and wanted to go back to their own bedrooms, so the Buckets said to Charlie and Mr WONKA, "We will take them to their respective bedrooms and will join you later. If we cannot find you, don't worry. Just explore the building by yourselves."

"Ok. Thanks." Charlie waved to his parents and then turned to Mr WONKA, "Let's go. Let's explore the basement and the underground tunnels.".

Once they entered the tunnel, they saw another tourist group in the basement and some other people wandering around. They must be overnight guests as well enjoying their self guided tour. The guide's soft voice could be heard from a distance, "The White House

Complex is protected by the United States Secret Service and the United States Park Police."

"NASAMS (Norwegian Advanced Surface to Air Missile System) were used to guard air space over Washington, D.C. during the 2005 presidential inauguration. The same NASAMS units have since been used to protect the president and all air space around the White House, which is strictly prohibited to aircraft."

Charlie and Mr WONKA had a quick tour of the basement. They noticed that there were quite a few heavy metal doors with signs which read "Access to the underground tunnels and hidden staircases are strictly prohibited!". With the daily access password which they acquired as special guests, they had no problem to open one of the heavy metal doors of the tunnels. The door looked massive, strong and solid, but slid to the side effortlessly as the required password was pressed.

Once they were in the tunnels, they saw more staircases and a long tunnel. They followed the tunnel and when they reached the end of the tunnel, there was a big enclosed space. To their big surprise, there was another White House which looked exactly the same as the one above the ground in the enclosed space.

"What's inside there?" Charlie seemed to be half asking himself and half asking Mr WONKA.

"We should take this opportunity to find out." Mr WONKA replied, not realizing that Charlie was talking to himself more than talking to him. "But how could we get in? I can see a guard walking around the building all the time."

"From what I can see, there is only one soldier constantly walking around it." Charlie said. "But let's wait for a while and see."

Both of them waited quietly but anxiously and after sometime, they found out they were right. There was only one soldier constantly walking around the building.

Charlie looked at Mr WONKA and said confidently and excitedly, "We can now easily find out who are in this White House and what they are doing there."

"But how?" Mr WONKA asked.

Charlie whispered to Mr WONKA, "When the guard turns around the corner and walks to the back side of the building, I will quickly run to the building and walk around it in the same direction and at the same pace as the guard does. In this way, the guard and I, who are always on the opposite side of the building, will never see each other."

"*Baumastic*, Charlie." Mr WONKA gave Charlie a thumb up. "Off you go. He has just disappeared and is on the other side of the building now. Make sure you walk a little faster than the guard because if you walk too slowly, the guard might see your back and catch you after a few rounds. But if you walk a little faster than he does, you can just wait at the corner and when he turns the corner at the other side, you can then turn around the corner as well."

Having no time to respond to Mr WONKA, Charlie quickly ran to the building and then started to walk around the building in the same direction but a little bit faster than the guard did while trying to peep inside the building. Sometimes, he could see the guard as he turned round the corner so he waited quietly until the guard turned his corner at the other side. To his big surprise again, he saw the President and the generals and the chiefs and his cabinet, all working hard inside the building.

"Isn't the President dealing with an emergency?" Charlie asked himself. "Or is he dealing with the emergency right here? Or has he changed his plan because the emergency has gone? Or has he finished and come back already?" Charlie's mind was running quickly as he kept on walking and peeping. He noticed that everybody inside the building had a computer in front of them with their own images and they were busy typing or sometimes saying commands to the computer. He tried to put all the bits and pieces together and began to see the complete picture. That might be one of the biggest secrets of the nation or of the world, but he had to wait to verify his guesstimation.

As soon as the guard disappeared at the back of the building, Charlie ran back to where Mr WONKA was waiting and they walked back to the basement where they saw another tourist group touring the basement. Then they walked up the stairs to get to the ground level.

"What did you see? Who were there and what were they doing?" Mr WONKA asked anxiously.

"The President and all his men. They were working inside the building." Charlie replied.

"What?" Mr WONKA exclaimed. "Weren't they having a meeting when we were touring with your parents and grandparents? Then the President had to excuse himself from the meeting to deal with an emergency."

"Yes and no. If what I guessed was right, then what we did at the banquet was futile."

"I don't get it." Mr WONKA looked confused and puzzled.

"I have to confirm one more thing to verify my guesstimation or deduction or whatever you call it. Then I will tell you." Charlie said.

Just then, they saw the President enter the building. "Have you dealt with the emergency already?" Charlie asked.

"Yes." The President answered. "I thought I would come back late in the afternoon but it didn't take me that long. In fact, I spent more time in my Cadillac than at the actual place. Enjoy your stay and see you later."

The President went back to his oval office to resume his work. Charlie said to Mr WONKA, "My guess was right. Let's go back to your bedroom and I will brief you."

As soon as Charlie entered the bedroom with Mr WONKA, he shut the door behind him and said, "Don't be shocked if I tell you that the President we just saw with our very own eyes is a robot. And so were all the generals and chiefs."

"My goodness! Can you say that again?" Mr WONKA couldn't believe his ears. He felt he couldn't believe his eyes either.

"The President we just saw is a robot." Charlie repeated. "That's why the President's voice we heard at the welcome ceremony and at the dinner was different in that it sounded as if he had a mild cold and there was an almost unnoticeable slight delay in all his responses. That's why there is a prohibited area in the basement. That's why I saw another President, the real human being, working in the other White House in the basement while the robot President went out to deal with the emergency. That's why I saw them typing and saying commands to their computers."

"The magic fudgemallow delights were made for human beings not for robots." Mr WONKA said, "My grandparents never thought of robots when they selected the ingredients. Although we can try to invent a new type of magic fudgemallow delights that will work for both human beings and robots but it will take a long time and we might not have another opportunity in our lifetime again to stay in the White House and be so close to the President or the Presidents."

"That means all our efforts had been wasted so far because it was the robots that consumed the magic fudgemallow delights at the banquet.

The magic fudgemallow delights would not take any effect on them. Human beings can control robots but not vice versa. We have to think of ways to meet the real President."

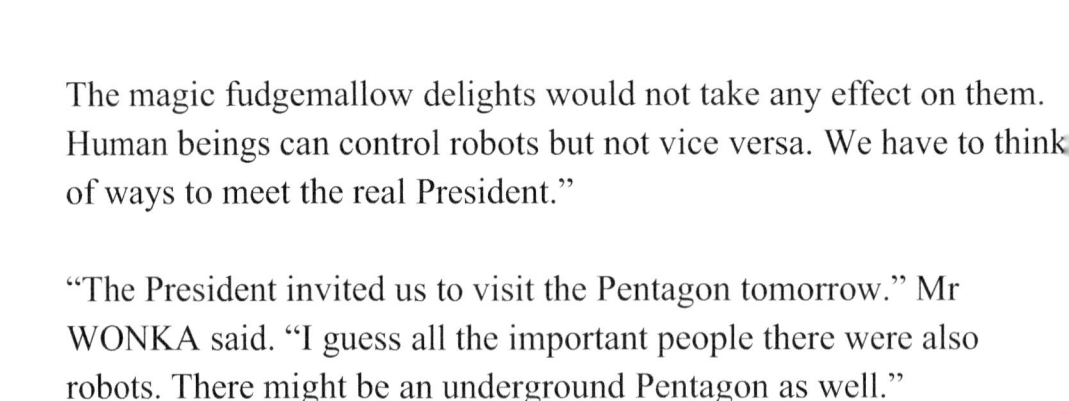

"The President invited us to visit the Pentagon tomorrow." Mr WONKA said. "I guess all the important people there were also robots. There might be an underground Pentagon as well."

"I totally agree." Charlie said. "Let's call it a day today and see if we can find some ways to meet the real President."

13 The Underground Pentagon

The Pentagon is the headquarters of the United States Department of Defence, located in Arlington County, Virginia, across the Potomac River from Washington, D.C. As a symbol of the U.S. military, The Pentagon is often used metonymically to refer to the U.S. Department of defence.

The Pentagon was designed by American architect George Bergstrom (1876–1955), and built by general contractor John McShain of Philadelphia. Ground was broken for construction on September 11, 1941, and the building was dedicated on January 15, 1943. General Brehon Somervell provided the major motive power behind the project; Colonel Leslie Groves was responsible for overseeing the project for the U.S. Army.

The Pentagon is one of the world's largest office buildings, with about 6,500,000 sq ft (600,000 m²), of which 3,700,000 sq ft (340,000 m²) are used as offices. Approximately 23,000 military and civilian employees and about 3,000 non-defence support personnel work in the Pentagon. It has five sides, five floors above ground, two basement levels, and five ring corridors per floor with a total of 17.5 mi (28.2 km) of corridors. The Pentagon includes a five-acre (20,000 m²) central plaza, which is shaped like a pentagon and informally known as "ground zero", a nickname originating during the Cold War on the presumption that it would be targeted by the Soviet Union at the outbreak of nuclear war.

On 11 September 2001, exactly 60 years after the building's construction began, American Airlines Flight 77 was hijacked and flown into the western side of the building, killing 189 people (59 victims and the five perpetrators on board the airliner, as well as 125 victims in the building). It was the first significant foreign attack on Washington's governmental facilities since the city was burned by the British during the War of 1812.

Neither Charlie nor Mr WONKA had a good sleep as both of them were thinking how they could meet the real President.

The grandparents didn't want to visit the Pentagon because they preferred to stay in their cosy bedrooms. The Buckets had an extremely difficult time to persuade them to go with them as you sometimes do with all the grandparents to go travelling with you. When the eight of them finally arrived at the Pentagon, they were truly amazed by its size and grandeur. The President, or to be more exact, the robot President, arrived shortly afterwards and they all went into the building from one of the sides.

"Good morning, Mr President! Good morning!" The guards saluted them as they entered and someone opened another door for them, "Welcome to Pentagon!"

"Is this a Pentagon or a triangular-shaped octagon?" Mr WONKA asked jokingly.

"This is where the Transport Capsule Control Centre is located." The President said with a smile. "This is also the control centre for all the chemical and nuclear weapons and all the missiles. Unfortunately I can only show you the former located in the lower level of the basement of the building."

They took a lift and as they were walking towards the centre, they passed a few doors which also had the signs that read, "Access strictly prohibited." That confirmed Charlie and Mr WONKA's guesstimation that there was also an underground Pentagon where all the chemical and nuclear weapons and all the missiles were operated and controlled by the U.S. Department of Defence.

"But Mr WONKA," Charlie pulled Mr WONKA aside and asked him quietly. "I heard there is an underground Pentagon in Pennsylvania already. Why is there another one down below here?"

"I will answer your query on our way back home." Mr WONKA replied and the two of them followed the President and Charlie's parents and grandparents already walking ahead of them .

The eight of them had a great time viewing the Transport Capsule Control Centre where the President spoke to them while they were in the Great Glass Elevator. Charlie sat on the very seat where the President spoke to them and even tried to imitate the President's voice, "*TODAY, THE ENTIRE NATION, INDEED THE WHOLE WORLD IS REJOICING AT THE SAFE RETURN OF OUR TRANSPORT CAPSULE FROM SPACE WITH 136 SOULS ON BOARD. ……*"

He then looked at the computer screens and asked a few funny questions, "How did the computer get sick?" Nobody from the Pentagon could answer it.

Grandpa Joe answered, "When it got a **virus** just as when I got sick."

"What do computers eat when they are hungry?" He asked again.

Grandma George replied, "**Chips**, which are also my favourite food."

"Which is our favourite key on the keyboard when we were travelling in the Great Glass Elevator?" He asked one more question.

Grandma Josephine responded without thinking hard at all, "The space bar."

Everyone had a good laugh. Then they had a tour of the other parts of the building until the grandparents felt tired again and wanted to go back.

After they had waved goodbye to the President and were on their way back home, Mr WONKA remembered to answer Charlie's query. "Yes, you are right. There is indeed another underground Pentagon in Pennsylvania, called the Raven Rock Mountain Complex (RRMC). It is an American military installation with an underground nuclear bunker near Blue Ridge Summit, Pennsylvania, at Raven Rock Mountain that has been called an 'underground Pentagon'. The bunker has emergency operations centers for the United States Army, Navy, and Air Force. Along with Mount Weather Emergency Operations Center in Virginia and the Cheyenne Mountain Complex in Colorado, it formed the core bunker complexes for the US Continuity of Government plan during the Cold War to survive a nuclear attack."

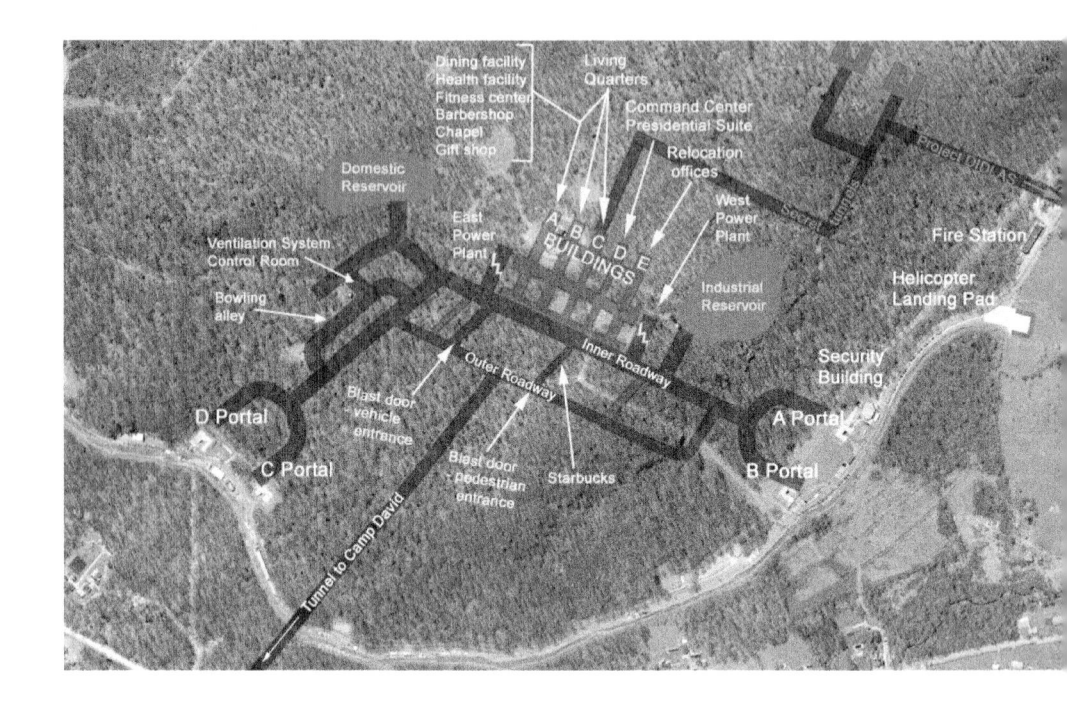

Charlie was all ears and Mr WONKA went on to tell him more about the complex, "The installation's largest tenant unit is the Defence Threat Reduction Agency, and RRMC communications are the responsibility of the 114th Signal Battalion. The facility has 38 communications systems, and the Defence Information Systems Agency provides computer services at the complex. Additional names for the installation are Raven Rock Military Complex, National Military Command Center Reservation (NMCC-R), 'Backup Pentagon', Site R, or 'The Rock'."

Charlie started to know the answer why there was another underground Pentagon in Pennsylvania. Mr WONKA continued, "RRMC is well known to the public as the Backup Pentagon and therefore is the attack target of all the other countries who intend to launch a war against USA. The underground Pentagon which we have just visited is the second or the real backup Pentagon."

By the time Mr WONKA had finished answering Charlie's query, they almost reached home as the Pentagon was only about six kilometres away from the White House. Once Charlie was in his own bedroom, he started to have some ideas of how they could meet the real President, but he had to discuss it with Mr WONKA first.

14 Starting All Over Again

Mr WONKA looked a bit tired as well as worried when he came back from the visit. He asked Charlie, "Have you got any good ideas for us to discuss so that we could find a way to meet the real President?"

"Vaguely." Charlie replied. "I would like to think a bit more before discussing it with you. I am starving and I want to have lunch now."

"OK." said Mr WONKA. "Let's have lunch and see if we can come up with a plan by dinner time."

After lunch Charlie told his parents that he was also tired and wanted to have a nap just like the grandparents. Only Mr WONKA knew that Charlie wanted to have some quiet and *sreme* time to think about the plan to meet the real President.

Charlie lay in bed for a long time, thinking hard. He finally had a rough plan but he wanted to receive confirmation and assurance from Mr WONKA.

He got up and knocked on Mr WONKA's door with some excitement in his eyes. "Come on in," said Mr WONKA.

"I have a query about the magic fudgemallow delights." Charlie got to the point straightaway. "We both know the robot or the fake President has taken the fudgemallow delights and so have the robot chiefs and all the real cabinet members in the right order. That means the next level down the line are the cabinet members but not the President or the chiefs as they were intended to be. If the real President and the chiefs and the cabinet take the fudgemallow delights again, will that change the order down the line?"

"Yes, of course." Mr WONKA confirmed. "The current order is me, you, then straight down to the cabinet if we ignore the pilot, because the President and the chiefs who took the fudgemallow delights are robots. If we can get the real President and the chiefs and the cabinet to take them again in the right order, this will wipe out the previous order totally and then we will have the desired order. But we still have the same old question: how can we get the real ones to take them?"

Charlie replied, "Because they are robots, I am thinking there must be a manual switch somewhere in their bodies that are not remotely controlled just in case. Just like the on/off switch of a TV, you must turn it on to activate the standby mode to make the remote control unit to work or turn it off to deactivate the standby mode. If we can turn off the switch of the robot President and then do some damages to it, the real one will definitely make his appearance."

Mr WONKA became excited about the plan, "But firstly, how can we know where the switch is located in his body? And secondly, once and if we know the answer to the first question, how can we do it? His bodyguard whom I suppose is also a robot is as strong as a bull and if we try to enter his Oval Office to do that by force, we might get killed."

"Answer to your first question, we can do some research to find out where the on/off switches are normally located in robots and then we can do something to confirm it. Answer to the first part of your second question, we will have to switch off the bodyguard first."

"But how can we and dare we switch off his bodyguard who is as smart and swift as a real professionally trained bodyguard?" Mr WONKA looked worried. "Surely we don't want to give him a fudgemallow delight."

"No, certainly not. But I think we can complete our mission when he has his fragile moment." Charlie said.

"What do you mean by fragile moment?" Mr WONKA had no idea of what Charlie was talking about.

"Just wait and see." Charlie gave Mr WONKA a grin.

"Let's get started then." Mr WONKA said. "Although the President said we could stay as long as we wish, we surely don't want to outstay his welcome, do we?"

"Of course not." Charlie agreed. "But first, let's do some research quickly to confirm where the switches are normally located in their bodies. From what I have read in science fictions and seen in movies, they are normally located on their back. Can you search some more and different types of robots and see where the switches are usually located?"

Mr WONKA went to the library and did a quick but quite thorough research and found out that Charlie was right. Most of the switches are located on the back although a few of them are located in the front or on the side.

"Let's get out there and check it out." Charlie said.

Mr WONKA went out quickly with Charlie who was holding a disposable cup of water in his hand. "Why do you want to bring a cup of water with you?" He asked quietly.

"You will see." Charlie gave him a mysterious look.

By that time they were near the Oval Office, they looked as if they were casually wandering through the place and were just walking past it. The guard standing near the Oval Office said hello to them and walked a few steps towards them and Charlie and Mr WONKA did the same. As they were about one or two metres away from the guard, Charlie somehow tripped over and all the water in his cup went splashing onto the bodyguard. Both Mr WONKA and Charlie said sorry to the bodyguard and *huratically* pulled up his suit and shook it as if they were trying to help him to dry up his suit. While they were doing this, they quickly touched the back of the bodyguard and found there was a hard plate there, the size of a small palm on the right side of his back. "I am so sorry." Charlie said apologetically. "I think I tripped over something and lost my balance."

"That's OK." The bodyguard went into the bathroom around the corner to dry his suit while Charlie and Mr WONKA returned to their bedroom.

"Now I know why you wanted to carry that disposable cup of water with you." Mr WONKA said. "Well done, Charlie. Now what next?"

"To turn off the switch of the bodyguard." Charlie replied without any hesitation.

"Why didn't you do that just now?" Mr WONKA didn't quite understand.

"That was not a good time. It will probably take a few seconds to complete the job. The bodyguard could have knocked me down in one second. Remember, he is a professionally trained bodyguard albeit a robot. I can only do it when he is at his vulnerable moment."

"When will he have his vulnerable moment?" Mr WONKA was keen to find out.

"I don't know. Will have to wait until that moment comes." Charlie replied. Mr WONKA was very confused but he didn't say anything more as he was sure that Charlie had already had a plan. "Do you want to have a drink?"

"No, I'm fine. Thanks." Charlie replied. "It is almost four o'clock. Tomorrow will be our last day. If we can get it done today, that will be great. Shall we go back again now?"

"Yes, but can you tell me the plan now?" Mr WONKA asked.

"I will signal you when the vulnerable moment comes." Charlie said with a grin as usual.

15 The Vulnerable Moment

Charlie and Mr WONKA went back to the place near the Oval Office. There was another tourist group stopping there while the guide was elaborating on the history of the building. The same bodyguard was still there and gave them a friendly smile and an affable nod. They pretended to be interested in the introduction by the guide and stood amidst the crowd to listen to the guide. When the guide finally finished his introduction and the crowd started to move in another direction, the bodyguard made his way to the bathroom around the corner. Charlie quickly gave Mr WONKA a signal and they both followed the guard into the bathroom.

The bodyguard either didn't notice that Charlie and Mr WONKA were following him or he did but just thought they wanted to use the bathroom as well. He opened the door, went in and started to loosen his pants which were obviously too tight and *nauvicious* for him to complete his business. Charlie and Mr WONKA entered the room in a flash and before the bodyguard could even say hello or smile or nod to them, Charlie pulled up his suit from behind. There he saw a panel on the right side of his back and on the panel with a red "ON" and "OFF" switch. Charlie quickly slid the switch to "OFF" and the bodyguard stopped moving and urinating immediately. All that, i.e. from dashing into the bathroom and pulling up the suit to switching off the bodyguard, was done in less than two seconds before the bodyguard could realize what was happening to take prompt reaction. Now the bodyguard looked really funny. He was standing right before the urinal, half turning with an astonished look and with his hands stuck in his pants, but he could not move any more, not even a single millimetre.

"Now I understand what you meant by vulnerable moment." Mr WONKA gave out a big laugh, still staring at the bodyguard. "But there is one thing I don't quite understand."

"What?" Charlie asked with a laugh as well.

"Since he is a robot, why does he need to make use of the bathroom?"

"Uha," Charlie said. "Just like the robot Mr President, if he consumes then he defecates. Sorry but we don't have time to discuss this because they would find out that the bodyguard had been disabled very soon. Let's go quickly to see the President."

"But we have to wait for his vulnerable moment to come." Mr WONKA reminded Charlie.

"No, we don't have to. He is not a professionally trained bodyguard and the two of us can easily disable him, I am sure." Charlie replied confidently.

The two of them pushed and moved the bodyguard to a urinal in the corner and turned him around to face the corner a bit. Although he was a disabled robot he was not a dead robot, his body was soft and gentle for them to restore him to the original position. He now looked as if he were using the bathroom.

Charlie and Mr WONKA came out of the bathroom quickly and went straight to the Oval Office where the President was working. They knocked on the door and Charlie said, "Hi Mr President. It's Charlie and Mr WONKA."

"Oh, come on in." The President replied.

They opened the door, let themselves in, and greeted the President again as they walked into the Office, "We are here to report something important to you."

"Yes, please. My special guests." the President replied with a pleasant look.

Charlie and Mr WONKA went up to the President and they were standing very close to Mr President now. "Well, you know …" Mr WONKA pretended to say something while Charlie dashed to the back of the President and tried to do exactly the same thing as he did with the bodyguard. But he couldn't see the panel on the back. The President got a shock and took a step back. "What are you doing, Charlie?" he asked suspiciously.

"Just to find out if you are the real President." Charlie said without any hesitation.

"Oh, no!" Upon hearing this, the President tried to resist the attack to the best of his capability but Charlie and Mr WONKA gave him no chance. They got him and pushed him down to the desk. Charlie quickly pulled up his suit again and found the panel on his left side. He *featomlessly* switched it off and the President stopped moving immediately and kept his bending position on the desk.

"Oh, Charlie." Mr WONKA said, "I am afraid that we can't leave Mr President like that in his office."

"Of course we can't. We will have to kill him." Charlie replied with a ruthless look.

"No, we shouldn't. Can't you turn on the switch, let him pose nicely and then turn it off again?" Mr Wonda looked worried.

"I am serious. We will have to kill him." Charlie repeated. "Don't worry! He is only a robot! If we don't kill him, the real President will never show up. Now hand me something that can chop or knock his head off."

"What about that flagpole?" Mr WONKA asked, pointing at one of the two flagpoles that held the Stars and the Stripes.

"That will do." Charlie said and taking the flagpole in both his hands, he smashed the panel attached to the body into 10 million pieces. "That will take them a while to fix that up." He said with a grin. "I am sure the real one will make his appearance in no time."

16 Talk with the Real President

"Beep, beep, beep, …" the computer in front of the President kept on beeping and a warning message kept flashing on the screen.

"We'll go and fix it, Mr President." A message immediately popped up on the screen.

"Oh, hold on. I will deal with it myself." The President responded immediately and left his seat and started to make his way to the Oval Office upstairs.

When the President went upstairs and opened the door, he saw Charlie sitting in his chair and Mr WONKA still trying to pull the robot President back to its position. "Don't worry about it." He then added, "They will fix him up in a minute."

"Hello, Mr President. We are so sorry for what we have done, but we just wish to meet the real President." Charlie and Mr WONKA greeted him simultaneously.

"Hello, my dear special guests." The President greeted them back with a twisted smile. "We need a good talk, don't we?" He signalled Charlie and Mr WONKA to sit down and another security officer who followed him quickly shut the door and exited the Oval Office.

"When did you start to make use of the robots?" Mr WONKA couldn't help asking.

"Well, back in the early 1980s when the Internet protocol suite (TCP/IP) was introduced as the standard networking protocol." The President replied without any hesitation.

TCP/IP Protocol Suite

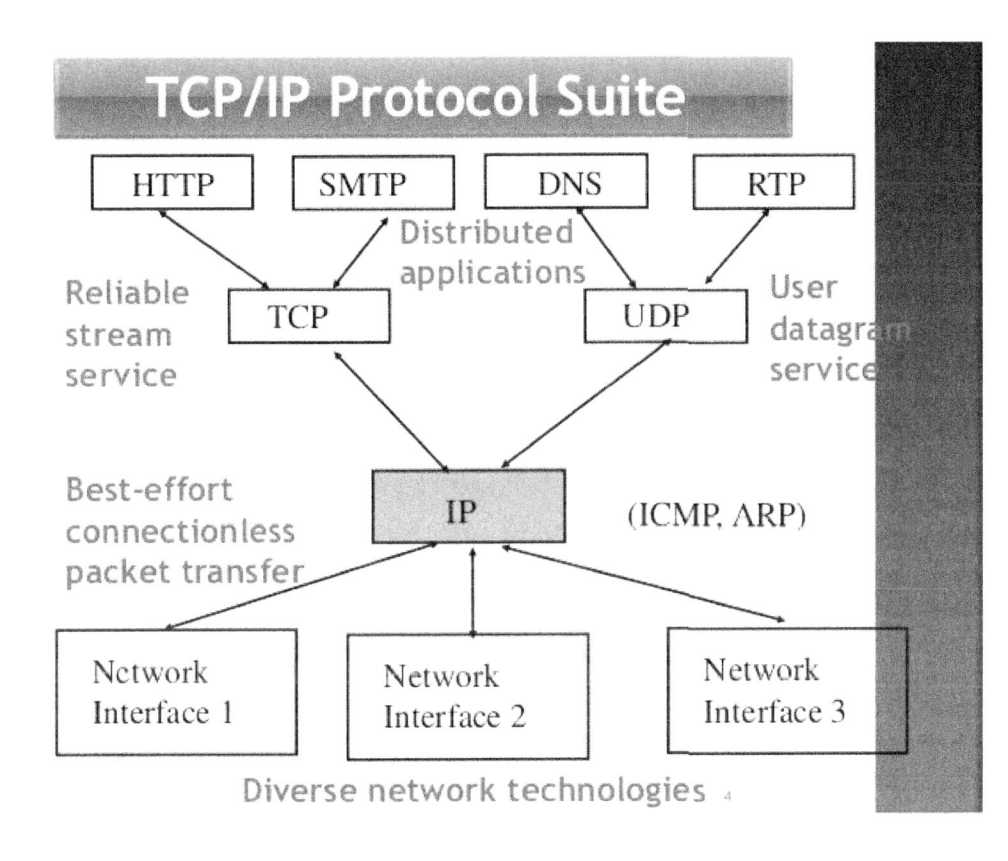

```
    HTTP      SMTP        DNS         RTP
                   Distributed
 Reliable          applications            User
 stream         TCP              UDP       datagram
 service                                   service

 Best-effort
 connectionless        IP        (ICMP, ARP)
 packet transfer

   Network          Network          Network
   Interface 1      Interface 2      Interface 3

         Diverse network technologies
```

"Why did you want to make use of robots instead of making your own personal appearance?" Charlie asked curiously.

"For obvious reasons." The President explained. "First of all, for the well known security reasons. Secondly, if I am away for whatever reason, the robot can always assume my role as the President. Thirdly, if we make an incorrigible mistake, for example, pressing the wrong button and accidentally launching a missile or a neutron bomb, then the robots can take the blame."

"Whose idea was that?" Mr WONKA asked.

"It's a collective idea. My brain can never produce such a brilliant idea." The President replied. "My doctor told me that **my left brain has got nothing right and my right brain has got nothing left.**"

"Hahahaha." Charlie and Mr WONKA could not help laughing.

"Being a politician and especially being a top politician of the nation is not easy." The President remarked. "I know a lot of people don't like politicians. They say '**Politicians are just like diapers. They need to be changed regularly and for the same reason.**' Do you agree?"

Mr WONKA said, "Agreed. I mean being a politician and a leader of the nation is not easy. **America is a country which produces citizens who will cross the ocean to fight for democracy but won't cross the street to vote.**"

Charlie asked, "**Why do Americans choose from just two people to run for president and 200 for Miss America?**"

"Haha. Good question." It was the President's turn to have a laugh. "Although this is my first year in the office, I need to start planning for the next election now. People say, '*If you fail to plan, you plan to fail.*' Do you know what a president does in his four years? He celebrates in his first year. He thinks about the next election in his second. He prepares for it in his third. And he runs for it in his fourth. Therefore he never gets anything done. I am really worried about the next election. I don't think I will be re-elected."

"Why?" Mr WONKA asked.

"Do you really believe in democracy? I don't. I didn't. I never have. And I never will. **In democracy, it's your vote that counts. In feudalism, it's your count that votes.** But just think of the funds involved to run an election campaign and just think of the immeasurable potential benefits those sponsors will receive if their preferred candidate wins the election."

"What benefits are you talking about, Mr President? I don't quite comprehend." Charlie asked with an innocent look which you can usually find on a boy's face.

"You are too young to understand this world, Charlie." The President said. "We are all connected and related. Our benefits are all linked and related. The sponsors receive their benefits through the laws and policies the politicians make. They don't sponsor you for nothing. I don't have enough funds to run for the next election. I don't like the sponsors who only wish to sponsor me for their own commercial benefits."

"I am sure Mr Wonda would like to sponsor you." Charlie said to the President, giving Mr WONKA a quick knowing smile.

"Yes, of course. We would like to sponsor you. We are not only your special guests, but would also like to be your special sponsors." Mr WONKA took over the topic. "And we are not seeking any personal gains. Of course, we do have a tiny request if it could be met."

"Please say it. Please." The President was eager to know what the request was.

"We would like to become the sole official supplier of fudgemallow delights to all government agencies, bureaus, departments and units. We will beat the price offered by the current suppliers by 5.432%. That is a massive saving of about 2.345 billion dollars a year for the government!" Mr WONKA quickly did his calculations in his head.

"A mutually beneficial business." The President said. "I like that. I take it."

"We do have another tiny request if it could be met as well." Mr WONKA said.

"Let me hear it, please." The President was keen to know what the second request was.

"We would like you and all the other officials who attended the welcome ceremony to hold another function to celebrate our deal in person. You know what I mean."

"That request can surely be met, my special guests and my sole and official supplier." The President replied without any hesitation or meapentredness.

"We have one last and final request, Mr President." Mr WONKA requested again.

"Yes, just let me know, please." The President was again keen to find out what the last and final request was.

"We would like to sign a contract for being the sole and official supplier for 16 years or for the next two presidents if they are re-elected whichever lasts longer."

"Well," the President hesitated. "That shouldn't be a problem during my term, but I cannot guarantee anything when the next president comes into office."

"It's hard to change the existing laws," Mr WONKA suggested, "but you can make new laws."

"True. Very true." The President agreed and shook hands with Mr WONKA and Charlie with a firm grip. "I will get the contract drafted tomorrow and we can all sign it at the function to celebrate the deal."

The President went to a cabinet, took out an expensive bottle of wine and opened it with a left handed corkscrew, which was one of his two inventions. (Do you still remember his other invention?) "Before you go, I would like you to have a drink to celebrate our deal here first."

He was humming to himself joyfully while pouring out the wine for
Charlie and Mr WONKA.

The real President has finally met Charlie and Mr WONKA
Who have discovered one of the top secrets of America
A mere lifelike robot is President Lancelot R Gilligrass
So is the cabinet and even his famous cat Mrs Taubsypass

There is another White House under the ground
Which is one of the secrets they have found
There is a backup Pentagon in Washington DC
Not the one known to the public as RRMC

Nobody wants to be assassinated like John Fitzgerald Kennedy
Who was pronounced dead in Parkland Hospital in tragedy
Who wishes to take the blame for starting the Third World War
If another nuclear bomb is accidentally launched like before

We have stricken a great deal about fudgemallow delights
Mr Wonda will supply them to the government day and night
There will never be any other better solution
To help me succeed in the next presidential election

The WONKA offer will beat the current quote by 5.432 percent
That is a massive saving of 2.345 billion dollars and one cent
I will provide them with free cars, petrol and accommodation
For them to supply fudgemallow delights for the whole nation

I cannot change the existing rules or laws
But I can enact new regulations and clauses
This is truly a mutually beneficial deal
All we need tomorrow is my presidential seal

Charlie said, "Sorry Mr President. I don't drink wine. I am too young to drink anyway. Even when I grow up, I still won't drink. I will probably just drink Fanta."

"For health or religious reasons?" asked the President.

"Both." Charlie replied with a chuckle. "But for another important reason as well. If I drink wine, people will say I am alcoholic, but if I drink Fanta, people will say I am **Fantastic**."

"Hahahaha. You are fantastic even if you don't drink Fanta." The President had a good laugh.

When Charlie and Mr WONKA finished talking with the President and returned to their bedrooms, Charlie asked, "Why do you want a contract to last for 16 years or for the next two presidents? That's way too long and I don't think I can live for 200 years."

"Remember our goal?" Mr Wonda asked. "To get rid of all the existing nuclear and chemical weapons and to achieve eternal peace and happiness in the world. This will not be done with one American President in four or eight years time. I know we and our offspring might be bound by this deal for 16 years. But it's worth it."

Before Charlie could reply, the telephone rang. "Hello!" Charlie picked up the receiver.

"Hi." It was the voice of the President's executive secretary, which sounded crisp and clear. "Mr President would like to meet you first thing tomorrow morning in his office. Please be ready by then."

"OK. Thanks." Charlie replied to the secretary. Then he turned to Mr WONKA, "Mr President would like to meet with us first thing tomorrow morning in his office. I wonder if he has changed his mind."

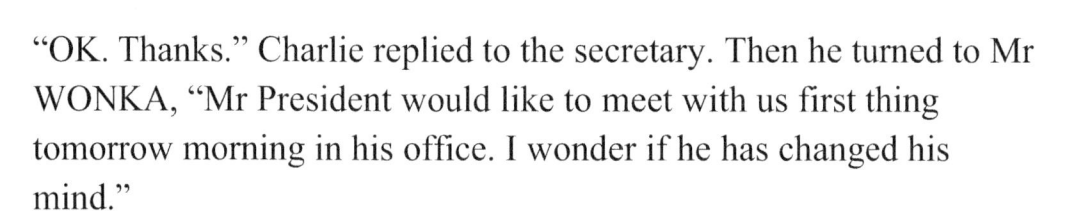

"No, I don't think so." Mr WONKA said with confidence. "There is no better deal than ours, I'm afraid. Let's have a rest and wait and see."

17 The Grand Decision

Early next morning, after another sumptuous breakfast, Charlie and Mr WONKA went to see the President who was already waiting for them in his Oval Office. He was busy fiddling the flytrap on his table, which was other of his two inventions.

After the normal formality of greeting and shaking hands with each other, the President pulled up his suit, "Have a look, the real President! No panel, no switches, no wiring. We have already fixed up the robot but I promise the real President will talk to you as long as you are here."

"That's great and thanks." Charlie said.

"I thought it would take at least a few more days to fix that up." Mr WONKA said.

"No, they did it in less than 6 hours." The President replied. "It is mainly the panel and switches and the wiring. The body was basically intact."

"Did you change your mind, Mr President?" Charlie asked, looking somewhat worried.

"No, I didn't." The President said. "In fact, I wish to talk more about our deal in details. It is a wonderful idea, a marvellous proposal, mutually beneficial, and I wish we could finalise the deal before you leave the White House."

"Sure. We know we put forward quite a few requests. Any requests from you President?" Mr WONKA asked.

"To be honest, I do have a request." The President replied without any hesitation. "I won't beat about the bush. I was wondering if you could all stay in Washington DC and manufacture your fudgemallow delights here. It will be much more convenient for us to contact each other in future. We will provide you with free accommodation, free food except chocolate from your factory, free cars and petrol, plus a very generous remuneration package."

"Thank you for the offer, Mr President." Mr WONKA said. "Personally, I would love to accept this very generous and tempting offer very much. But I think we'd better talk to Charlie's parents and his grandparents first before we accept your offer. Could we get back to you this afternoon or tomorrow morning the latest?"

"Sure. Have a think about it and I look forward to hearing from you very soon."

Charlie and Mr WONKA went back to see Charlie's parents and the grandparents and told them about the offer made by the President.

"We don't have to worry about shelter and food anymore! We will live for 120 years like Moses, **the first person with a tablet downloading data from the cloud!**" Mr Bucket cried.

"We will be living like kings and queens and princes and princesses!" Mrs Bucket shouted.

"I want to go back to my home. I don't like this place." Grandpa Joe yelled.

"I don't like to see so many buildings and so many people and so many cars here. I can't even breathe." Grandma Josephine screamed.

"What about your chocolate factory?" Grandpa George asked.

"Who will look after the oompa loompas?" Grandma Georgina queried.

"We are all leaving! We are all going back!" The grandparents said in chorus.

"Do you want to have some more time to think about it?" Mr WONKA asked. "We can let the President know tomorrow morning."

"No." The grandparents said again adamantly in chorus. "We all want to go back. This is the decision made by all the grandparents. It is a **grand** decision."

'If you are 100% sure of the **grand** decision, Mr WONKA and I will go back and report to the President right now." Charlie said.

Charlie and Mr WONKA went back to see the President, who was surprised to see them back so soon. "Do you have more questions?" He asked surprisingly.

"No. We are back to tell you about the **grand** decision. We do have some concerns with regard to your offer. Charlie has got parents who have got grandparents to look after. I don't think they would like to stay in Washington DC, especially the grandparents, who were asking all the time when they could go back home. What's more, the fudgemallow delights should be made from 100% organic ingredients, which can only be produced from remote places with no pollution at all. In addition, I and/or rather Charlie still have the chocolate factory to look after in the near future. There are lots of other constraints as well, so I am afraid we might not be able to meet your request."

"Totally understood." The President said. "My offer will always remain open. If you do change your mind, please let me know and I will make necessary arrangements accordingly."

"Mr President." Charlie said. "Thank you so much for your invitation and generosity. My grandparents would like to go back as soon as possible so we are thinking of leaving tomorrow morning. And we certainly don't want to outstay your welcome."

"Pleasure. You are welcome to stay as long as like." The President said. "If you insist on leaving, I would like to host a farewell dinner tonight."

"Thank you." Charlie said. "Will let the rest of the family know. And see you tonight at …?"

"Seven o'clock." The President replied.

Charlie and WONKA went back to spread the news. The grandparents were ravished to hear that they could leave the following morning.

"Charlie." Mr WONKA asked. "Can I talk to you for a second?"

"Sure." Charlie replied and went with Mr WONKA to his bedroom.

"I am really tempted by the offer." said Mr Wonda. "Too good to be true. I almost bought it and wanted to stay. But I am worried that all our conversations in future, even our conversations now, are monitored and recorded. That's why I always whisper to you if I have something important to tell you. Now, tonight is the night. But I am worried they might use the robots again. You can never trust those politicians."

"True. I know a little boy who always tells lies to his parents and friends and classmates. When asked what kind of job he would be competent to do when he grew up, he replied either a politician or a meteorologist. Haha"

"So we need to come up with a plan to make sure that those who attend the farewell dinner tonight are real people not robots."

"I have already got a plan." Charlie said, looking as calm as a cucumber. "Just wait and you will see."

"I trust you, Charlie." Mr WONKA said. "Now let's have a break and have some lunch."

18 The Farewell Dinner

The dining hall was nice and warm and *doukid*. The farewell dinner started at exactly seven o'clock as the President said. The menu followed the similar pattern of the welcome dinner. It was a great relief to Charlie and Mr WONKA that all the important people who attended the welcome dinner were present. Charlie was wondering how all of them could gather together in such a short notice and how they could all arrive on time.

"Taxpayers' money." Mr WONKA said. "In this country, there are two things that nobody can avoid."

"What are they?" Charlie couldn't help asking curiously.

"Death and taxes." Mr WONKA replied. "Don't you know taxes pay for the majority of business class and first class of airlines as well as for overtime and other allowances for politicians? Now are you ready for action?"

"What action?" Charlie knew what Mr WONKA meant but he asked him on purpose.

"I am just asking how they would show us they are real politicians not robots. You are not going to pull up or pull down their suits one by one in the middle of the dinner, are you?" Mr WONKA looked worried.

"Just relax, Mr WONKA." Charlie replied with a grin. "Of course I am not. They will have to show me themselves very soon. Don't you worry."

"Ok. I trust you Charlie as always." Mr WONKA looked less worried now, but still looked puzzled.

The temperature in the dining hall was nice and warm when the dinner started but now it seemed to be much higher than before. Some of the invited guests started to take off their suits. At this moment, the voice of the master of the ceremony sounded clearly and *deevily* in the dining hall. "Attention, please. The President would now like to make his farewell speech."

"Ladies and gentlemen." The President started his speech, holding a microphone in his right hand, which was the wrong hand as he was left handed. "I have had great pleasure of having the eight national heroes as our special guests for the past few days in the White House. They are all departing tomorrow morning. On behalf of the whole nation, I would like to express my gratitude to them once again."

By that time, the dining hall was scorchingly hot, unbearably hot, one should say. Almost all the guests had taken off their suits. The President was perspiring as badly as the three chief commanders. He took out a handkerchief to wipe his forehead and the three chiefs did the same.

"See, Mr WONKA.' Charlie whispered. "They are robots. The temperature is almost 30 degrees and they still have got their suits on."

"Now I see. But when did you change the set temperature of the air-conditioning?" Mr WONKA asked.

"I did that just before we entered the dining hall." Charlie replied proudly. "I spent the whole afternoon playing with it and figured that out. I set it to warm up to 30 degrees for half an hour before they could reset the temperature just to see if they would take their suits off."

The President was concluding his speech by the sound of it. "To quote William Shakespeare, who is a better wordsmith than I am:

And whether we shall meet again I know not.
Therefore our everlasting farewell take:
For ever, and forever, farewell, friends!
If we do meet again, why, we shall smile;
If not, why, then this parting was well made."

Everybody applauded as loudly as they could and the President returned to his seat. While he took out another handkerchief to wipe his face, Charlie went up to him and said, "Mr President, we would like to see the real President and your real chiefs here today."

The President looked startled and replied, "I AM the real one!"

"I can understand that you wanted to wear your suit while you were making the farewell speech to be formal, but there is no reason why you are still wearing it now that you have concluded your speech.

Please go and get the real President and the real chiefs. We would like to see them back in shirts and ties."

"Excuse me!" The President was really trying to find an excuse now. "Excuse me!" He said to the audience, in a loud voice. "The chiefs and I have an emergency matter to discuss with each other. Please excuse us for about 10 minutes." He signalled to the chiefs and they hurried out of the dining hall.

"Well done, Charlie." Mr WONKA gave Charlie a wink.

"Hopefully, they will return in shirts and ties this time." Charlie whispered to Mr WONKA with a giggle.

19 Contract for Fudgemallow Delights

The real president and the chiefs returned in about ten minutes as they promised. They were all dressed in shirts and ties. No one noticed any differences except Charlie and Mr WONKA.

"I will now ask someone to turn the temperature down." Charlie said to Mr WONKA with a grin.

"You look much better in shirts and ties guys." Mr WONKA said sarcastically.

"Thank you." The President said awkwardly and embarrassingly.

"Let's enjoy our dinner and then you may announce the news before we have desserts." Mr WONKA said.

"Thank you for reminding me." The President said.

"Could you pass me the drink, please, Mr WONKA?" Charlie asked. "I am as thirsty as a walrus due to the high temperature."

The dinner was coming to an end and the President stood up again. A microphone was promptly handed to him. He cleared his throat and said with his usual booming voice, "Ladies and gentleman. It is with great pleasure that I announce Mr WONKA's or now Charlie's Chocolate Factory will form a strategic partnership with us from now on. They will be the sole official supplier of fudgemallow delights to all government agencies, bureaus, departments and units. They will beat the price offered by the current suppliers by 5.432%. That is a massive saving of about 2.345 billion dollars a year for the government! The agreement will be signed and witnessed just before our special guests departing tomorrow morning. Excuse me but I can only use the "F" words to describe this achievement, i.e. it is fascinating, it is fantastic, it is fabulous! To celebrate this great deal, I propose a toast. Cheers!"

"Cheers!" The sound echoed in the dining hall.

"As expected," the President's *geriatric* voice could be heard again as the resonance in the dining hall subdued, "We will still have the fudgemallow delights as our desserts tonight. Please enjoy the rest of your dinner and the desserts will be served very soon."

"Charlie, my good gracious Charlie!" Mr WONKA leaned over to Charlie and whispered into his ear. "We have messed up everything again. We had so many other things to worry about and we forgot all about the magic fudgemallow delights. What shall we do now? I am not worried that we won't have fudgemallow delights for desserts tonight, but worried that the real president and the chiefs won't have them tonight. And consequently, all our efforts have come to nothing. We are stuck. We are finished."

"Don't worry, Mr WONKA." Charlie said in his calm voice as usual. Everything will be alright."

"I do worry. I am worried to death." Mr WONKA looked really worried. "Don't tell me you can feed all those people with the remaining fudgemallow delights as Jesus did to the multitude with five loaves and two fish. You cannot perform miracles. Don't tell me we can go back again to make more of them. We don't have time. Don't tell me you brought some extras. I know you didn't."

"Seeing is believing." Charlie said. "Just wait and see for yourself."

Just then, the waiters and waitresses started to serve the desserts. They were exactly the same ones they had at the welcome dinner except that they were a bit smaller. As previously arranged, the President had the privilege and honour to take the first bite followed by the three chiefs and the rest of the cabinet.

The President and the chiefs stood up to shake hands with the special guests. "Excuse us, but we have to leave now to discuss another important matter. Enjoy the rest of the night. We will see you tomorrow morning. Good night!"

Once the President and the chiefs were gone, the grandparents wanted to leave as well. When they were all back in their bedrooms, Mr WONKA couldn't help asking Charlie, "Where did the magic fudgemallow delights come from?"

"From the chocolate factory." Charlie replied with a grin.

"But how? Who made them?" Mr WONKA asked curiously again, determined to find out the truth.

"They came with us in the helicopter and we made them." Charlie replied with a smile.

"But there wasn't much left after the welcome dinner!" Mr WONKA still had that puzzled look on his face.

"True." Charlie replied. "Do you remember the leftovers? I asked the chefs to remake some more magic fudgemallow delights out of them. That's why they are a bit smaller in size but just enough for the President, the chiefs and the cabinet. The ones for the other guests are not special magic fudgemallow delights although they didn't taste much different."

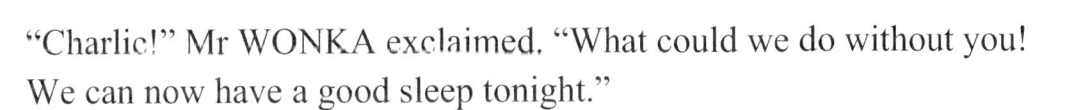

"Charlie!" Mr WONKA exclaimed. "What could we do without you! We can now have a good sleep tonight."

"Yes. Good news or bad news? I heard the same pilot would fly us home tomorrow morning. I also heard the pilot would like to find something very different to do when he retires. Hope that won't ruin our plan."

"Let's leave tomorrow's worries to tomorrow." Although Mr WONKA said looked relaxed, he became worried again about the pilot.

20 Flying Back Home

Everybody woke up early on the day of departure and started to pack up the belongings. The grandparents were so excited that they could go home.

Grandpa George said, "If you have a biological clock, you will never need an alarm clock."

Grandma Josephine said, "I woke up at 3:30 this morning and couldn't go back to sleep again."

Grandpa Joe said, "I think I have packed up everything."

Grandma Georgina asked, "Can we go now?"

"No, not yet." Mrs Bucket said. "Mr WONKA and Charlie have to go and sign the contract first."

"Yes, that's right." said Mr Bucket. "You go and we will wait for you."

Charlie and Mr WONKA hurried to the Oval Office where the President and some other relevant officials were already waiting for them.

While Mr WONKA was browsing the contract, the President interrupted unintentionally, "Mr WONKA, I do realise that some of the clauses were not written into the contract. I believe you understand the contract is based on mutual trust and goodwill."

Mr WONKA knew that the President was referring to the sponsorship to his election, "Yes, of course. We have already reached an oral agreement. Please rest assured that the contract will come into effect on the starting date and be carried out as stated."

Mr WONKA signed on the contract after the President put his autograph on it. Everybody applauded and the President shook hands with Mr WONKA and Charlie, "Congratulations! Have a good trip! All the best."

"Thank you, President. Good luck" Mr WONKA said.

"Thank you, Mr President. Best wishes." Charlie said.

Both of them shook hands with the other officials who were present at the ceremony while numerous cameras were flashing one after another to capture that special moment.

By the time Charlie and Mr WONKA went back to their bedroom, the pilot, the same pilot who flew them to the White House, was already helping the grandparents load their luggage onto the helicopter.

"How are you doing?" Mr WONKA greeted him. "I heard that you will pursue something very different when you retire very soon."

"Vely well, thanks." The pilot answered. "Don't be surplised if I tell you I will lun for the next plesidential election. I have always been interested in politics and have always wanted to become a politician.

Charlie and Mr WONKA were so taken aback that neither of them could utter a single syllable. They could not **bear** to look at this **bear looking** pilot who took the magic fudgemallow delights a few days ago. After all, it was probably not wrong for him to take the magic fudgemallow delights anyway.

Charlie and Mr WONKA have signed the contract with the President
To become the sole supplier of fudgemallow delights
They have successfully completed their mission up to the present

To bring to all the nations peace and love and no fights

The President and the Vice President and his cabinet do not know
That their middle brains have already been alterated
If they wish to start another World War like the one many years ago
Even their whole bodies and brains might be refabricated

The parents and the grandparents are happy to go back home
In their new elegant clothes bought in the shopping mall
They will enjoy their normal life without any fearful syndromes
With endless supplies of sweets and chocolates for them all

Charlie and Mr WONKA will be the real leaders of USA
To make new rules and laws for the whole country
Rules that will benefit the people in their own way
And laws that are fair, just and elementary

They will support the pilot to run for the next presidential election
Although he was not born in USA and speaks a second language
As long as he is righteous and works for the whole nation
As long as he is fair and just and can totally manage

They will make more special fudgemallow delights
And they will bring them to every corner of the world
Who knows who will be the next person to have a bite
And what mysteries and secrets they will unfold

References

Charlie and the Chocolate Factory by Roald DAHL
Charlie and the Great Glass Elevator by Roald DAHL
First chapter of Charlie and the White House by Roald DAHL
The Magic Finger by Roald DAHL
Fantastic Mr Fox by Roald DAHL
George's Marvellous Medicine by Roald DAHL
Esio Trot by Roald DAHL
James and the Giant Peach by Roald DAHL
The BFG by Roald DAHL
The Witches by Roald DAHL
A Literary Viewpoint: Charles Dickens visits the White House
Letter from John Adams to Abigail Adams, 3 July 1776
www.roalddahl.com
The White House, Wikipedia
Mid brain, Wikipedia

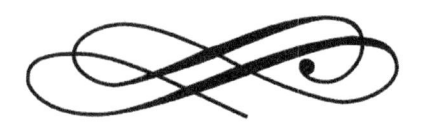

About the Author

Yaoxiang WANG was born and brought up in Shanghai China. He started to learn English at the age of eleven in a primary school in Shanghai. When he was thirteen years old, he was selected to study English at Shanghai Foreign Language School, a boarding school attached to Shanghai Foreign Language Institute now called Shanghai International Studies University (SISU).

Upon graduation and obtaining his Bachelor's degree in English Linguistics and Literature at SISU, Yaoxiang was invited to teach English at SISU for two years and a half before he went to study International Economics at Nankai University in Tianjin China. He returned to SISU and taught Economics there for about half a year after he had completed his postgraduate study in Tianjin.

Yaoxiang went to Australia to pursue further study in 1989. He received his Master's degree in Information Technology and Management at University of New South Wales and taught Chinese, Information Technology and English as an Additional Language (EAL) at Copland College in Melba Canberra now called Melba-Copland Secondary School from 2001 to 2005.

Yaoxiang taught EAL at Secondary Introductory English Centre in Dickson Canberra from 2006 to 2016. It was there that he was first exposed to Roald DAHL's stories (contrary to what he said at the beginning of this novel). He was so fascinated by DAHL's novels, especially his manipulation of the English language as well as his creativity and great sense of humour that when he found out that DAHL only finished the first chapter of "Charlie and the White House" after reading "Charlie and the Chocolate Factory" and "Charlie and the Great Glass Elevator", he had a burning desire to finish this long awaited novel, no matter what it took.

Yaoxiang started writing "Charlie and the White House" in the middle of 2016 and completed the draft at the end of the year. As he was working full time during the day, he spent most of his evenings and Saturday mornings on writing the novel, constantly reminding himself of the seven tips from Roald DAHL on the qualities he thought necessary to anyone who wants to make a living out of writing fictions, i.e. (1) have a lively imagination, (2) write well, (3) have stamina, (4) be a perfectionist, (5) have strong self-discipline, (6) have a keen sense of humour, (7) have a degree of humility and most importantly, have an attractive plot.

Being a very versatile person, Yaoxiang has a variety of interests and hobbies including classical music, cooking, gardening, languages, drumming, poetry, reading, dubbing, magic tricks, religion, financial literacy, and of course, the Chinese culture. He works and lives happily with his wife and children in Canberra where he has been living and working since 1989.

Other books (Wong boks) by Yaoxiang WANG

- Funny English
- English Grammar in 7 Days
- My Superb Stunning Short Stories
- Best Jokes of the World

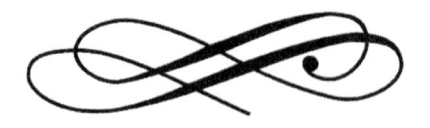

End of the book